Taboo Collection
By Selena Kitt

Table of Contents

Sibling Lust: On the Bus ...………...……………...…….....   1
Sibling Lust: In the Fold ...………...……………...…….....   13
Sibling Lust: In the Barn ...………...……………...…….....   24
Sibling Lust: Under the Stars ...………...……………...…….   32
Daddy's Favorites: Darla...………...……………...…….....   48
Daddy's Favorites: Tina...………...……………...……....   63
Daddy's Favorites: Anna...………...……………...…….....   86
Daddy's Favorites: Christa...………...……………...……..... 103
Daddy's Favorites: Clara...………...……………...……..... 133
Daddy's Favorites: Becca...………...……………...……..... 157

On the Bus (Sibling Lust)

"Do you know why animal crackers have that little handle on top of the box?" Danny asked, nudging his stepsister with his knee.

"No," Emily sighed, putting her own book down and switching off her reading light, waiting. There was no use doing anything else—he was going to tell her, whether she wanted to know or not.

"They were introduced in 1902 as a Christmas novelty and packaged so they could be hung from Christmas trees," he said, reading from the book in his lap.

"How interesting." She rolled her eyes. It had been like this all day, and now halfway into the night—a constant stream of interruptions with various bits of trivia. She hadn't even made it off the fourth page of her own book!

"How many different animal shapes are there?" he asked, cocking his head at her.

"I don't know," She closed her eyes and leaned her head back against the seat, feeling the rolling wheels of the bus underneath them chewing up the miles between here and California. "Twenty-seven?"

"No!" he scoffed. "Eighteen—two bears, a bison, a camel, a cougar, an elephant, a giraffe, a gorilla, a hippopotamus, a hyena, a kangaroo, a lion, a monkey, a rhinoceros, a seal, a sheep, a tiger, and a zebra."

"Okay, seriously, Danny." She shook her head but didn't open her eyes. "Alex Trebek is not going to ask you about animal crackers."

"You never know," he said, sounding hurt.

"Yes, I do." She ignored the tone in his voice, pushing onward. "Jeopardy asks questions about the periodic table and Queen Victoria, not snack foods."

"Fine." He jerked himself toward the window. "I'll just shut up and leave you alone."

Emily smiled, still not opening her eyes, breathing, "Finally!"

It was quiet only for a moment before he spoke up and asked, "What does the chemical symbol Fe2O3 represent?"

"Danny!" She groaned, slapping her forehead. "I have no idea! I'm not the Mensa member here."

"Rust," he replied, looking smug. She hit him in the arm. "Hey! I'm just trying to expand your horizons a little!"

"I don't need my horizons expanded." She got up and flounced off to the bathroom.

Emily splashed her face with water, pushing her hair out of her eyes. Her eyes were blue and bright, like her mother's. Danny, on the other hand, was dark eyed and dark-haired, like his father, the man Emily had called "Daddy" until she was twelve. He hadn't been, of course, and Danny wasn't really her brother, only by marriage, both of them coming along as a package deal when Emily was just a baby and her mother recently widowed.

This is his fault, Emily thought, scrubbing her hands fiercely. If only her stepfather hadn't ever moved out to California in the first place. But off he'd gone, leaving Danny behind, leaving all of them.

She sighed, turning the hand dryer on. When she'd agreed to this cross-country trek to visit Danny's father, mostly so her younger stepbrother could to try out for Jeopardy now that he'd reached the eligible age of eighteen, she hadn't counted on having to listen to Danny "practice" for hours on end. She loved the kid—but come on! There was only so much trivia one person should be forced to listen to, wasn't there?

He was turned toward the window when she got back, looking at something on his video iPod. She flopped into her seat, digging through her backpack for her own.

"I'm sorry." Danny apologized without looking up.

She softened, hearing his hurt tone. "It's okay... I'm just... you know, not looking forward to swallowing the whole Dad and his new wife and kids Happy Family Meal..."

"Yeah," he agreed, rolling his eyes. "No doubt."

"Damnit, I left my headphones in my suitcase." She sighed, tossing her iPod back into her bag.

"Do you want mine?" Danny asked. "I'm just reading..."

"Reading? On your iPod?" Emily made a face. "Don't you listen to music and watch videos like normal people?"

"Just more research." He shrugged, not meeting her eyes.

"I'm sorry, Dan." She apologized again, touching his arm. "I didn't mean... what are you reading?"

"Porn," he replied, still not looking at her.

She laughed. "Very funny."

"Well, it's not really..." he admitted, giving her a sheepish grin. "It's just an e-book of useless sexual trivia."

"More trivia, huh?" She smiled, shaking her head.

"It's interesting," he said. "Did you know the tapeworm has the most sexual organs of any living being?"

"Oh gross!" She groaned, hiding her face in her hands. "Danny, please!"

"Okay, okay." He grinned. "How about this... How many orgasms do you think was the most ever recorded for a woman in twenty-four hours?"

Emily cocked her head at him, frowning. "I don't know... nine? Ten?"

His smile grew. "A hundred and thirty-four."

Her eyes widened. "Oh my god! I'd die!"

"For guys it was only sixteen... although I swear I've beat that..."

"Danny!" Emily hissed his name, glancing around at the sleeping bus to see if anyone was listening.

"How many for you?" he asked, looking at her speculatively.

"I don't know." She shrugged, biting her lower lip. She had the distinct feeling she shouldn't be talking about this with her stepbrother. "Probably five... maybe six..."

"Lightweight." He winked. "But you guys... or gals, I should say... get to have longer orgasms. A man's climax only lasts ten seconds, tops... girls have had orgasms for nearly a minute..."

Emily squirmed in her seat. "Dan... let's change the subject..."

"Why?" He gave her a sideways look. "You want to talk about animal crackers some more?"

"No!" she protested. "Okay, fine, tell me more sex trivia..."

"There are only five calories in the typical male ejaculation."

"Oh good god!" she laughed. "That's a good reason not to swallow!"

"Eh, not really. Sexual intercourse burns about three hundred and sixty calories."

"Well, at least I can say I'm multitasking..."

"Did you know a woman's nipple can swell up to twenty five percent when she's aroused?"

Emily flushed. "Is that so?"

"Well, that's what it says..." Danny's eyes moved over the front of his stepsister's blouse. "And this is kind of neat... there's a tribe on one of the Cook Islands where boys of a certain age are actually taught how to have sex... everything from intercourse to cunnilingus, and methods for delayed ejaculation..."

"Like... hands on?" Emily swallowed, wiggling in her seat.

"I think so," he nodded. "Which, when you think about it, could be really useful..."

She nodded. "I can see that... most of the guys I've been with..."

When she trailed off, he glanced over at her. "Yeah?"

"Well... let's just say, they could've used some instructional techniques."

"Yeah." Danny sighed. "I could've used some too."

Emily looked at her brother, a little smile on her face. "I bet you do all right."

"I'm a geek." He shrugged. "Geeks don't get the girls, you know."

"Ha!" She nudged him with her shoulder. "What about that Sarah girl last year? I saw you guys in the pool that summer..."

Danny flushed. "Yeah? Well... you should have closed your bedroom door when you and Max were... ya know... getting busy..."

Emily felt her face fill with heat. "Dan! You didn't..."

He shrugged, busily studying his iPod.

"I think we should try to get some sleep," Emily whispered, reaching up and turning off his reading light. The screen of the iPod still glowed in the dark.

Emily reached under her seat and grabbed the sleeping bag she had packed, snuggling underneath. The rocking of the bus, which should have lulled her off to sleep, seemed to vibrate through her body, making her feel on edge. Still, she gave it a valiant try, only succeeding in tossing and turning in her seat.

"I can't sleep, either," Danny whispered in the dark, shifting in his seat.

Emily sighed. "Here, do you want covers?"

Danny accepted the other half of the sleeping bag, pulling it over his shoulders. "Are you thinking about Dad?"

"No," she admitted.

"Me, either," he replied.

There was a long silence as the bus traveled on in the dark. Someone coughed. Up front, another light turned off.

"What were you thinking about?" Emily whispered.

There was another silence. Then, Danny said, "You."

She closed her eyes, taking a deep breath. Part of her wanted to know—another part of her didn't. "What about me?"

"Remember that time when we all went camping in the mountains?"

"Yeah." Her memory tuned to it, as if finding the right frequency or channel. Ninety degrees in the shade and they were sleeping in one tent, while their parents shared the other. Both of them had slept naked on top of their sleeping bags in the dark, although Emily remembered being careful to get dressed before the sun rose.

"It was so hot... remember?"

She nodded and, although he couldn't see her in the dark, she knew he somehow felt her assent.

"There was one morning when you went down to the creek to take a bath and I followed you..."

"Danny..." It should have come out as an admonishment, she meant it to, but instead it was just his name, almost tender on her lips.

"I was just thinking..." he whispered. "I don't think I've ever seen anything so beautiful..."

"That was before they got divorced," she said, touching his hand under the sleeping bag. "Before everything changed..."

"I know." He squeezed her hand. "I love you, Em."

"I love you, too," she said.

"Come here." He pushed up the seat divider and reached for her. Emily moved in to snuggle against him. It just felt right somehow, in that moment. He held onto her, stroking her hair, and they both drifted off to the rocking motion of the bus.

She dreamed about the mountains—splashing naked in the creek, the cold water a shock to her body as she splayed herself against the smooth rocks on the riverbed. The rushing water flowed over her belly and breasts, and she

spread her legs like she was fucking the whole world, letting the rushing foam pulse between her thighs.

Had she known he was watching? In her dream, she knew. He was standing there, transfixed, looking at her like she was a goddess, and that's just what she felt like. Letting her long hair fan out in the water behind her, she gave herself over to it, to him, to everything, opening herself to the world.

"Emy..." It was a whisper, his pet name for her, leftover from when he couldn't quite say his L's.

In her sleep, she shifted, the Birkenstocks she had worn in honor of their California trip left somewhere on the floor, her long skirt riding up her thighs as she snuggled closer to him in the dark.

"Oh, god, Emy..." His breath in her ear made her shiver, and she came out of her dream in a haze, finding herself curled around her brother, her breasts pressed against his side, her thighs over his.

"Danny?" she whispered, realizing she was practically sitting in his lap. His hand was resting on her knee, his other arm holding her close. He didn't answer her, and she gazed at his sleeping face, knowing he must be dreaming.

She kissed his cheek, smiling, wondering what he was dreaming about. His expression was almost pained in the dim light, and he whispered her name again, shifting and pressing his hips up in his sleep. That's when she knew. He couldn't hide anything in the sweats he had worn for the long trip. When she felt his erection against her bare thigh, she gasped softly, her eyes widening.

Emily flushed, moving slowly, trying to disentangle herself from him in the dark. He instinctively held onto her tighter, his hand sliding further up her leg, gripping her thigh. Her heart raced, and she didn't want to admit it, but there was a slow heat growing between her legs where the edge of his hand was resting. His face was buried in her hair now, his breath hot against her ear, making that thick pulse between her thighs even more insistent.

"You're so beautiful, Emy," he whispered, his lips moving over her cheek, and now the hand between her legs moved too, fingers moving lightly over the damp crotch of her panties.

"Danny," she whispered again, and for the second time today, words that should have been an admonishment came out as something else. It sounded like a plea. *Oh my god, what's he doing?*

She shifted, trying to get away or get closer, she wasn't sure which, and he pulled her fully into his lap, settling her bottom against the saddle of his hips. She could feel his erection—my god, he felt huge, like steel heat against her behind. He cradled her like that, kissing her neck as his fingers edged aside the elastic edge of her panties.

"We... Danny, we..." Her whispered words were lost as his lips found hers. This was no brotherly kiss. His mouth was hot, slanting across hers, his tongue probing gently, like his fingers between her legs.

Trembling, Emily tried to force herself to resist, to get up and run to the bathroom, and found she couldn't. Maybe it was the way his finger began nudging the swollen bud of her clit, or the way his tongue flicked at hers, sending shivers down her spine.

But that wasn't really it, and she knew it. It was the heat of his cock against her ass, how incredibly hard he was. He had been dreaming about her, she knew it, and the thought excited her. His fingers moved around her clit in lazy circles, and she spread her thighs a little, giving him more room.

When she slid a hand down between them, pressing the head of his cock against his lower belly, Danny groaned softly, his breath hitching in his throat. It made him bolder, and his finger slipped down her smooth, shaved crevice, seeking entrance. Emily worked her fingers past the elastic edge of his sweats and under the top edge of his underwear, wanting to feel him. She had to feel how much he wanted her.

"Oh god," she whispered against his cheek when his fingers slipped inside of her and he settled his thumb against her clit. "Oh yes..."

"Yes," he murmured, making a soft noise in his throat as she wiggled in his lap, her hand finally reaching its destination and squeezing the head of him. The shock of it in her grasp sent a jolt through her whole body—she was holding her brother's cock in her hand!

His fingers began to move slowly in and out of her wetness, making a soft, squelching sound. Emily glanced around, worried someone would hear or see, but the man across the aisle was snoring, his head propped on a pillow resting against the window. Danny's thumb rubbed over her clit as his fingers probed her flesh, making her rock in his lap.

"Faster," she whispered in his ear, trying to grasp more of his cock, but the angle was too awkward. She had to satisfy herself with rubbing the wet head with her thumb.

Danny began pistoning his fingers in and out of his sister's pussy, and she spread her thighs wider, her breath coming fast. Emily surprised them both when she untied the top of her peasant blouse, reaching in and unfastening her front hook bra, and presenting her brother with one pink-tipped breast.

"Suck it." Her voice was barely audible, but he didn't really need any instruction. His tongue made circles around the hardening flesh, and Emily let out a shaky breath as he sucked her nipple deep into his mouth.

The added sensation threatened to send her careening over the edge, and she arched her back. Emily tried hard not to cry out as her brother's fingers, driving into her wet flesh, brought her to the brink of orgasm. She succeeded, for the most part, making a small, squeaking noise in her throat as she came, her whole body shuddering against him. Danny held her tight, one hand on her hip, the other bringing her off with such force she nearly bucked off his lap.

"Danny," she gasped into his ear, and he kissed her, drawing her tongue deep into his mouth, his fingers still probing the sensitive flesh between her thighs.

"Emy, I want you," he whispered, kissing her cheek, her neck, her chin. She bit her lip when his fingers slipped from between her legs, and watched, her eyes widening, as he licked them. "God, you taste good."

In the wake of her orgasm, she had a moment to think clearly, and felt a flush of shame. This was her stepbrother! Danny rubbed his wet fingers on the tip of her breast, making her shiver. His cock was still pressing up hard and insistent against her behind, and when she rubbed her thumb there, he made a low noise, his eyes closing for a moment.

"Please, Em," he whispered, rubbing his finger over her mouth. "I want you so much."

She had never been able to say no to him, and she couldn't start now. Emily kissed his palm, and then took one of his still-sticky fingers into her mouth, sucking gently. She squirmed and adjusted for a moment, reaching under her long skirt and tugging off her wet panties. Part of her couldn't believe she was doing it, but another part of her wanted it beyond reason as she straddled him in the dark.

"Is this what you want?" Emily whispered into his ear, glancing again at the sleeping man across the aisle. He had shifted position, but was still snoring. Danny's fingers were fumbling with the front of her blouse, freeing both of her breasts to his gaze, and his touch.

Danny just nodded, his thumbs flicking over her nipples, making her squirm in his lap. Emily reached down, tugging at the edges of his sweats, and he helped her, moving them down far enough to free his cock. It rose like an exclamation point against her belly, she could feel the heat of it against her mound.

"Do you want to feel your cock inside of me?" she whispered, meeting his eyes. They were full of a dark, hot lust. He nodded again, his breath coming a little faster as she reached down to stroke him against her pussy. He groaned

softly when she rubbed the head up and down her slit, finally aiming him, and slowly beginning to settle herself down.

"Ohhhh fuck," he whispered, his hands under her skirt, grabbing onto her bare hips. He pulled her in tight, and Emily watched the look of almost unbearable pleasure move over his face.

Something occurred to her, and she asked, "Have you ever fucked a girl before?" She kept her mouth right near his ear, afraid someone might hear them if she raised her voice above a whisper.

He shook his head, his breath short and his hands moving over the smooth, rounded globes of her ass, his hips already thrusting slowly against hers. The shock of his response made Emily dizzy with lust, and she squeezed her pussy around him, like a reward, making his fingers dig deep into the flesh of her behind.

"Come on, Danny," she murmured, rhythmically squeezing him, now. "Fuck me."

He groaned softly at her words, rocking his hips up to meet her. She knew it wouldn't be long, but it didn't matter—just knowing she was the first girl her little brother had ever fucked had already sent her teetering toward that edge. His movements were awkward, and she took over, rolling her hips on him, using the wet heat of her pussy to pleasure the head of his cock now buried deep inside of her.

"That's it, baby," she crooned softly, feeling the gentle tug in her lower belly beginning. "Fuck me good... fuck your sister's tight little pussy 'til she comes all over your hard cock."

"Oh yeah," he growled into her ear, thrusting up hard into her wetness, the tight heat of her pussy beginning to spasm with her climax. "Oh, Emy, I'm gonna come!"

The sound of her pet name in his mouth, the baby name he'd always used, while her brother's cock exploded inside of her, made Emily come even harder. She arched her back,

taking all of him, feeling the thick, incredible bursts of heat in her belly as he filled her with his cum.

Still trembling and breathless, they snuggled close, pulling the sleeping bag fully around them as the bus rumbled on in the darkness.

Emily kissed her stepbrother's cheek, pushing a curl off his forehead. "Wanna tell me some more trivia? Practice for Jeopardy?"

Danny's eyes were closed, but he smiled. "I think I've found something I like practicing more."

In the Fold (Sibling Lust)

Abby spent the morning with the little ones, teaching them their ABCs and 123s. I didn't know how she could stand it, wiping snotty noses and putting on thirty pairs of shoes when it was time to go outside. She seemed good at it though, a natural. I saw them when I was coming out from gathering eggs, following her in a long line, like she was a mother duck and they were her ducklings. It made me laugh, and I waved at her, but she frowned and shooed me back to my work.

I spent the afternoon in the kitchen, and Abby came to join us after lunch, when it was time for all the children to go into the chapel. I felt sorry for them. Daddy Zeke hadn't instituted Children's Chapel Time until after Abby and I were old enough to join The Hands, so we never had to sit with our fists under our chins and our feet tucked under us for two hours under Brother's Jim's watchful eye. I couldn't imagine having to sit still for so long, even now.

"Rachel, pay attention," Abby whispered, pointing to where I was cracking eggs into a huge mixing bowl. We cooked for the whole compound, ten us of prepping everything for the Kitchen Hands, and there were a hundred and seventy-eight of The Hands of God total at last count. We were supposed to work in silence, although we often didn't.

"What?" I grabbed another egg. "You're making me lose count. Eight, nine, ten…"

"You've got shells in there," Abby said, kneading the dough on the bread board. "If Daddy Zeke gets a shell in his eggs, you're going to be sorry."

I sighed, fishing the little bits of shell out that I could find. "Picky, picky."

"Not me," she said with a shrug. "Him."

I glanced over my shoulder as if he might be there, although I knew he was in seclusion, either napping or preparing for the service. It was almost time for afternoon prayer. I finished counting out the eggs, beating them and adding the onions, green pepper and tomatoes I had picked from the garden just this morning and cut up before Abby came in.

"Hurry, Rachel," Abby urged, taking off her apron and hanging it on a hook. She washed her hands in the sink behind me while I slid the huge tray of eggs, ready for tomorrow's breakfast, into the double-wide refrigerator. "We don't want to be late."

I sighed, stepping in beside her to wash my hands too. Around us, everyone was finishing their prep work, in a hurry to get to afternoon service. I hung my apron up too, and followed Abby out of the kitchen and down the hall. We both knelt in front of the altar at the entrance, bowing our heads and hastily whispering a rote prayer to the picture of Daddy Zeke hanging above it.

"Our father, whose love is infinite and complete, I offer my hands and my heart to you in service for the greater good."

Behind us, other Hands were lining up to say their own prayer before exiting the building. There was an altar at every entrance and exit on the compound. We all whispered that prayer hundreds of times a day.

Abby and I rushed out of the building, hurrying without running in our full black skirts. I saw her tucking her long blonde hair up under the white kerchief tied over her head. We weren't allowed to cut our hair, but we also weren't

allowed to let it show in public. I checked my own, making sure it was tied tight behind my head.

The Sanctuary was already half-full. We slipped our shoes off—the kitchen was the only building that allowed shoes—and knelt and prayed again at the entrance, moving toward the front to find our seats. Every seat in the sanctuary was assigned, and Abby and I sat near the front, because we were Zeke's daughters. My mother, Mary (her real name was Sophie, but she took a Biblical name when she met Zeke) had died seven years ago, just after Abby and I turned twelve. Abby's mother...we just didn't know. No one would ever say who she was. They had simply said Abby was abandoned, and Daddy Zeke and Mother Mary had charitably taken her in, a newborn along with their own tiny baby daughter, and raised us like twins. We even looked so much alike people often mistook us for the same.

The front row was filled with Zeke's wives, and those of his children who were twelve and up—old enough to be baptized into the Way of the Hands of the God. The little ones were still in the chapel, I knew. Abby sat, hissing at me to sit next to her.

I sank into my seat, still staring across the aisle at a man who I'd never seen before. His black robe and his thick, dark curly hair made it clear that he was a preacher—all the male Hands shaved their heads at puberty and wore white button-down shirts and black trousers and only while working in the sun did they wear their wide-brimmed black hats.

He smiled and inclined his head toward me, and I smiled back without thinking.

"Ow," I whined when Abby pinched my thigh, rubbing it and staring around her anyway at the man, who now held a Bible open in his lap. Definitely a preacher. None of the Hands were allowed to have Bibles. Our Word came from the pulpit. We were simply the Hands of God.

I heard the big doors close behind us, signaling the beginning of the service. We bowed our heads and folded

our hands. We were supposed to close our eyes in five minutes of silent prayer, but I kept sneaking glances at the preacher man.

He was young. Not as young as we were, but young, still. It was strange to see a man with hair. I had never seen a full grown man with hair, except Daddy Zeke. Looking at the way it curled at his neck made me want to touch it. I just knew it would feel silky and soft.

"We are the Hands of God."

The chant began, and I joined with them, taking Abby's hand and Dinah's next to me. I was wishing I had sat on the end, because Abby got to reach across the aisle and touch the hand of the preacher man as we chanted, louder and louder, the sound of our voices filling the sanctuary.

Just when our voices reached their pinnacle, raised in fervent supplication, the door behind the pulpit opened and Daddy Zeke strode in. There was an immediate silence as Daddy grabbed the pulpit on either side with his big, wide hands, closing his eyes and bowing his head. I was always so amazed that Abby didn't look anything like him—all dark curly hair and eyes and wide, broad features.

Of course, neither did I. He said we were china dolls with our fine blonde hair and wide blue eyes, pale and delicate features. Abby had one picture of her mother (cameras weren't allowed on the compound) from their wedding day, and Abby and I look just like her, as if she were our twin too.

"He has set you upon the path to righteous freedom." When Daddy Zeke began to speak, it was like a small earthquake tremor starting. I knew, because we got a lot of those out here in California. "You are the Hands of God."

"We are the Hands of God." The sanctuary spoke with one voice.

"He has given you two hands to serve him, and with just those hands and your open heart, you can have your salvation right here in this moment. Do you believe me, brothers and sisters?"

"Amen!" the congregation murmured. On the other side of me, Eli, who had just been baptized and accepted as a Hand last week, was whispering something to little Sara. Zeke's eyes fell on him and Eli felt them, turning back up to the pulpit, red-faced. There was very little that Daddy ever missed. I had learned long ago never to do things I shouldn't in his presence.

"He holds the world in his hands!" Daddy Zeke held up his hands to us, his palms facing out. "And I say, you hold the world in yours! Every time you fold your hands in prayer, every time you offer your hand to your brethren, every time your hands work in service for Him, you follow your path toward deliverance!"

I leaned a little forward and slid my eyes past Abby, looking at the preacher man. He was holding his Bible and nodding his head, along with the rest of the congregation. I couldn't, for the life of me, figure out who he could be. Daddy Zeke was the only preacher we had ever had, that we had ever known. He was the reason The Hands of God existed in the first place.

I must have gotten lost in my daydreams, because the next thing I knew, Daddy was saying, "I want you to extend your hands to my son, Malachi. He is to be our new preacher-in-training."

The congregation was humming and swaying, holding their hands above their heads in approval. I did too, but I looked at Abby with wide eyes.

"He's the son of my first wife, Ruth, bless her and keep her. He's my bloodline, and he's the sole lineage to the Hands of God. Please welcome Father Malachi."

The dark-haired man stood, moving toward the pulpit. Abby's thigh was tight against mine, nudging me, and I nudged her back. He was older than we were, maybe by five years. How was this possible? Daddy Zeke was married before? If it was so, no one had ever spoken of it.

"Thank you," Malachi spoke, his voice like liquid gold compared to Daddy's rough timbre. His dark eyes met mine

and I saw the resemblance immediately, with them standing side by side like that. "I've long been called to this work, and I only ask for God to give me the strength in my own hands to lead you on your paths as Hands of God."

"We are the Hands of God! We are the Hands of God!" The chanting began again, and I joined in, hearing the tremble in Abby's voice as she did, too. Our hands were raised to them, but she hooked her pinky finger over mine, and I understood that she was as shocked and scared as I was. I knew we would talk about it later, but for now, we bowed our heads and raised our hands in worship.

* * * *

Abby and I had slept in the same bed since we were babies. Our little room was next to Daddy's at the back of the house, and we still shared the twin bed we always had. Daddy had offered to put us into separate rooms, but we refused. The rest of the house was filled with his wives and their children, and I often felt out of place with them, like an outsider. Abby and I had our dark little cocoon at the back of the house and that's the way we liked it.

"Daddy says he's been living in seclusion since just before you were born," Abby whispered in the dark, her breath sweet against my face. We had both picked an apple to eat on the way back from evening service, where Mal (as he told us to call him) had officially been welcomed into the fold with his Homecoming.

"But why?" I kicked the covers off my feet. It was too warm in here. "And where?"

"I don't know."

We were quiet for a moment, and I could feel her belly rising and falling against mine. I remembered the way Mal had squeezed my hand and reached over to hug me. He did the same to Abby, really acting the long-lost brother. Daddy looked so pleased that I tried to look happy, and Abby did too. My face hurt from smiling.

"I wanted to touch his hair," I whispered and Abby giggled.

"I wanted to touch more than that," she said, putting her hand on my hip and pulling my belly fully against hers.

"Abby!" I was aghast. "He's our half-brother!" Although, technically by blood, he was really only mine. We never thought of each other as anything but sisters.

She giggled again. "Well, I didn't know he was our brother when I was thinking about it."

"Well... you're my sister." I could feel her breasts pressed against mine now, mirrors of my own, small and pointed and pink-tipped.

"That's different," she whispered, stroking my cheek, brushing my hair out of my eyes. It was only at night that we could let our hair free. We should have braided it, as neither of us had ever cut our hair and it hung past our bottoms. We often woke in a tangled blonde mess in the morning.

"Why?" I asked, feeling her thighs against mine, the familiar ache between my legs.

"We're girls, silly." She tilted my chin up and kissed me. She tasted like apples, clean and sweet and delicious. Her tongue found mine and I moaned softly, reaching between my legs and cupping my mound, as if I could stop the ache there, although really I had discovered only one thing that could.

Abby took my hand and placed it between her legs and I rubbed her through her long white nightgown, little electric jolts running through my body from every contact point with hers—her hand on my breast, her tongue and lips against mine, her other hand pulling my nightgown up and stroking my thigh.

She rolled on top of me then, straddling me and lifting her nightgown up over her head, tossing it to the floor. Her hands edged mine up too, the material rubbing across my nipples, making me shudder. Then her mouth was there, sucking and licking at them, and I could feel the heat of her wetness as she rocked her mound against mine. It was

always such a delicious tease, her lips rubbing against mine like that. It made me moan and whimper.

"Shhhh," Abby urged, kissing her way down my belly. "Don't wake Daddy Zeke."

"Ohhh!"My voice was barely a whisper as I spread my thighs for her, feeling her parting my lips with her fingers, her tongue searching and finding that tender, swollen bud at the top of my cleft.

It was just last year she taught me how to rub it in fast little circles until I was breathless and dizzy and thought I was going to die. First, I watched her do it, leaning back against the wall with her legs open in this very bed, saw her head go back and her eyes close, heard her moan and then saw her whole body flush and shudder. It made my breath come fast and something throbbed between my legs.

So I did it with her, both of us rubbing there, rubbing and rubbing until I thought I couldn't stand it anymore, that I was going to burst or die or—and then one day it felt like I did die, when the whole world exploded into a burst of delicious, pulsing white light and heat. I called it Heaven, although Abby said one of the Hand boys told her that it was called "coming." Once it happened, I couldn't get enough of it.

Abby's tongue moved back and forth over that sweet, sensitive spot, and I rubbed my palms over my nipples, sending pleasure waves down through my belly toward my hips. Everything was centered where her mouth was licking and sucking, soft, wet friction that made me wiggle and pull at her hair, wanting more.

"Come here," I whispered. "Let me do you too."

I'd been so scared the first time I tasted her, not knowing what it would be like. She did me, that first time, telling me one of the Hand boys had done it to her one day way out in the orchards. It was a sin, a horrible, awful sin, although she swore he hadn't put anything inside of her. We still wouldn't put anything inside the virginal space for fear of being deflowered.

After her tongue had sent me to the most intense, astonishing, breathtaking Heaven I'd ever been to, I'd felt obligated to do her too. She said I didn't have to—but I did. Now, I loved to taste her—it made me even more excited, feeling her flesh against my tongue, tasting her sweet juices as they ran down my chin.

Abby moved her slender thighs over me, spreading her legs as she positioned herself. I grabbed her hips, pulling her against my mouth, licking and sucking, wild and unrestrained. It made her moan against me, sending waves of divine pleasure humming through me as she continued her exploration between my legs.

Her tongue flicked faster and faster and I made small noises in my throat, urging her on as I licked her little, swollen spot, back and forth, again and again. She was making noise now too, and I loved her noises and how her thighs tightened and her hips rocked, using my tongue for her pleasure.

I found myself fast approaching the gates of Heaven. It wasn't a sweet, slow spiral upward anymore, now I was flying, racing headlong toward exquisite release. When Daddy talked about freedom and salvation, I thought this was what he meant, this journey toward ecstasy.

Abby's tongue and mouth were a soft, wet, glorious push. I moaned and twisted underneath her, wrapping my arms around her hips and feeling her mash herself against my face, my tongue buried in the folds of her flesh until I could barely breathe, but I didn't care.

It started like Daddy's sermons, like a small earthquake, rumbling through my pelvis and shuddering my hips as I bucked and arched. Abby made little noises, knowing the sound and feel of me at my pinnacle, licking faster than ever. I gasped and moaned and forgot about her spread over my face for a moment, lost completely in my own paradise.

"Rachel," she whispered, her fingers moving there, still, sending jolts through me, and I put my whole mouth over her in thanksgiving, rolling with her until she was on her

back. She gasped and wiggled, her breath fast and her hips rocking as I licked and licked and licked. Her hands gripped my bottom, her nails digging into my flesh, but I didn't care. I could hear her making that "ah, ahh" noise she made when she was close.

"Oh God, Rachel!" she cried, gripping my hips and arching her back. She quivered under me, her belly convulsing, undulating, the little bud of flesh under my tongue pulsing with her pleasure. I didn't stop, still teasing her with my mouth until she begged.

"I can't stand it," she cried, half-laughing, half-sobbing as I flicked my tongue over that sweet, sensitive spot.

Finally, I turned around to her and we kissed, the taste of our flesh mingling in our mouths. She didn't taste like apples anymore, but she still tasted sweet. I retrieved her nightgown, and pulled mine down, snuggling back into bed and pressing my behind back against her hips, never imagining that it might be one of the last times we ever did this.

"I love you," Abby whispered, draping her arm over my side.

"I love you too," I whispered back, closing my eyes, still tasting the sweet juices of my stepsister in my throat.

"I have to tell you something." I heard a catch in her voice that made my eyes open in the dark. "Daddy Zeke has decided. I'm going to be married."

"What?" I stiffened, and then relaxed, laughing. "Don't joke, Abby!"

"I'm not joking." She kissed my shoulder and then pressed her forehead there with a shaky sigh. "I'm to marry Malachai next month."

"I can't believe it." I felt a tight ball of coldness clenched in my belly at the thought, along with a hot streak of jealousy. I knew I shouldn't feel that way. He was my half-brother, after all—but he wasn't hers. Not by blood. So this was how Daddy Zeke would continue his empire after

he was gone, how he would bring more members into the fold.

Abby choked out her words. "I don't want to lose you."

"You won't lose me." I turned and took her into my arms, knowing that our bonds, blood or not, could never be broken. "I'll always be your sister."

I saw his face that night in my dreams, our new preacher, Mal, and I wondered about him, holding onto Abby as she drifted off. I knew we couldn't run away together or fight what Daddy Zeke wanted, but I was determined to make sure of one thing—I wouldn't ever let anyone separate me from Abby. We would be sisters—and lovers—forever, no matter what.\

In the Barn (Sibling Lust)

My adopted brother masturbated in the barn, way up high in the loft, lying alone in the soft, clean hay we shoveled down for Da to feed the animals. I didn't understand at first, what he was doing. I think he would have heard me, that first time I climbed up the ladder, ready to tell him Ma needed a hand moving something in the kitchen, if he hadn't been about to make a mess. I saw him, lying down, black hat tossed aside, head cocked at a funny angle, and at first I panicked, thinking he was hurt. But then I heard his fast, labored breathing, saw his hand moving between his legs, and knew he was holding onto his privates.

But what could he be doing to them?

I stood frozen on the ladder, eyes wide, as his hand moved faster and faster, like lightning, up and down. He gave out a soft moan, his hips bucked up, and I stared, shocked, as thick, white streams shot over his fist, up onto his bare belly, where he'd pulled up his shirt.

I knew it was a sin. It couldn't be anything but. Instead of confronting him that first time, I snuck down the ladder as quiet as I could. I told Ma I didn't feel well—and no, I didn't find Eli in the barn, I said—and went to my room, which was really mine and Ada's and Becca's together.

I felt sick, remembering what I saw, but I was curious too. What could he have been doing with himself like that? The sounds he made were sort of like he was in pain...but

why would he be hurting himself? And at the end, the shock of the liquid shooting from his privates…it wasn't pee. I knew what that looked like. My littlest brother, Isaac, had peed on me enough during diaper changes for me to know the difference.

I lay there a long time, feeling funny down low in my belly, playing the scene over and over in my head. Eli was the eldest, in his twenties now, me just behind him, turned eighteen last spring. He was Ma's sister's boy really, but when my aunt died of sepsis soon after he was born, Eli's father had left our order, too full of grief to stay, and the baby had stayed too. My parents had raised him as their own and we had known each other as brother and sister from the beginning. I knew I shouldn't have watched him, knew I shouldn't be feeling the way I was, but I couldn't seem to help myself.

That's when I decided to watch Eli, to see if he did it again. It was the next afternoon he disappeared from the side of the house where Da had him stacking wood. I was hanging laundry and saw him head to the barn, so I followed.

This time, I saw it all, from beginning to end. I peeked over the top of the ladder to watch, even untying and taking off my white cap—a sin in and of itself—hoping the darkness of the barn would hide me, and let my brown hair blend into my surroundings. If he looked over, he would only see that—the top of my head and my wide eyes. I watched him lie back in the hay, unfasten his pants, and start touching his privates.

It was soft at first—a small snake in a nest of hair—but the more he touched it, the bigger it got. I stared, aghast, when it stood straight up, more than double its original size. Eli licked his palm, calloused from hard work, and wrapped his fist around the length, moving his hand up and down, just like the day before.

His breath came faster and faster—and so did mine. That funny feeling was back in my belly, low down, cradled

in my pelvis. Something ached there, throbbed, like a tooth does, only it wasn't a hurtin' sort of agony, but a delicious kind. I wanted more of it. And the more I watched, the more the feeling swelled until I felt like I was going to burst.

It wasn't long before he was moaning again, whispering, "Oh, oh, oh!" and then shoving his privates up into his fist, the thick white stuff flooding out the end. There was so much of it!

I didn't go to my room this time. Instead, I hurried down the ladder and went back to hanging laundry, but the gnawing tickle took a long, long time to go away. Eli's hand touched mine when I asked him to pass me the milk pitcher during dinner and I thought the heat rushing through my torso would make me faint. He gave me a funny look, but I just kept my eyes down and finished eating.

Still, I didn't stop watching. I couldn't. I felt compelled, even though I knew it was a sin, I knew the devil was in me, and I had to rub him out. I tried. I did. I stood on the ladder, watching my brother pump himself like he was a well, waiting for the blessed moment when the liquid finally surfaced, and I lifted my long skirts to touch myself too.

I didn't have what he had. Girls and boys had different parts, I knew that much from changing diapers for Ma when the babies needed it, but I never knew how complimentary the parts were, how different and yet how similar. I pressed myself there over my undergarments while I watched him, worrying myself between the legs again and again. I knew if someone came into the barn—if Da had come in…my blood curdled just thinking about it.

But he never did. And one day, when Eli was thrusting up into his hand and I was at my usual spot on the ladder, watching, I felt the little tickle between my legs build to a sneeze. Something had to give. My fingers moved, back and forth, around and around, my whole body tingling with sensation, and then…it happened.

The world exploded.

I cried out—I couldn't help it—my whole body trembling with the force of the devil inside of me, and I wondered briefly if I had finally driven him out. My legs wouldn't hold me. They turned to jelly and I fell, catching myself halfway down only to lose my grip again and land, hard, on the dirt floor below.

"Sarah!" Eli was calling. I was okay, but dazed, breathless, still stunned by what had happened, and I didn't answer him. He took the ladder two rungs at a time, sweeping me up over his shoulder and carrying me back up like I was a sack of potatoes.

When he had me on the hay, touching my face, calling my name, I finally opened my eyes. He was concerned, but embarrassed too, and I knew he was wondering how much I'd seen. *Oh, Eli, I've seen so very much,* I thought, catching his hand and bringing it up to my heart.

"I know it's a sin," I whispered, lifting his fingers to my mouth and kissing them. "But I can't help it."

"Help...what?" His dark, puzzled eyes met mine, and I searched his earnest face with my heated gaze.

"I saw you," I admitted, feeling the heat move into my cheeks. He flushed, too. "Eli, it was so wonderful!"

"Sarah, I'm sorry." His eyes dropped to the hay. "It is a sin. I shouldn't. I need to stop. I know you'll have to tell Ma...or Da."

"No." I swallowed hard at the thought and cradled his hand against my cheek. "I don't want to tell."

"But..."

"Something that feels so good can't be a sin," I insisted, half sitting now, back on my elbows. "It can't possibly. I just...I understand now. Why you keep doing it, how the whole world opens up for a moment and you feel like you're dying, or flying. I felt like I could touch God himself."

He was staring at me, wide-eyed. "How long were you watching?"

"I've watched lots of times." I lifted my chin, defiant, in spite of my flushed cheeks. "I touch myself too."

Eli gaped. "Where?"

I hesitated before slowly placing a hand between my legs, over my long skirts. "Here."

Puzzled, he frowned. "But you don't have…"

"I know." I shrugged. "But it feels good, all the same."

His eyes brightened, still focused between my legs. My hand still rested there. "Will you… show me?"

Stunned, I stared at him for a moment, unable to breathe. The sort of sin I'd committed so far was nothing compared to what he was asking. Only babies were allowed to be naked in front of others. I looked into his eyes, saw the eagerness, the hunger there, the longing I felt too, and slowly I started to lift my skirt. His gaze followed its path, up my knee-sock covered calves, and then my bare knees. He gasped when he saw those, his eyes following the path of my skirt up my bare thighs until I had it pulled up to my waist.

Then I pressed my hand between my legs, over the heated, damp mound there, and began to rub myself. He watched, fascinated, his breath coming almost as fast as mine.

"Have you ever taken these off?" he whispered, tugging at my undergarments.

I shook my head, my heart hammering in my chest.

"Will you?" he breathed, his eyes meeting mine. What I saw there made me want to do anything, anything at all for him. "Oh Sarah, please."

The desperation in his voice moved me and I tugged them down and off. The air over my privates was cool, and I explored with my fingers a place I had only touched through my clothes, or when I quickly washed myself on Saturdays. The sensation was incredible, so intense, my fingers growing wet as I parted the dark hair and probed in between.

"That's so lovely," he breathed.

"Do you like it?" I asked, glancing down at my parted thighs, the dark triangle.

He nodded, eyes transfixed, and I saw his hand rubbing his privates again through his breeches.

I rubbed the most tender spot, finding a little nub of flesh there I hadn't felt before through my clothes. Touching it made me moan, and my breasts felt suddenly heavier. "It feels so much better without my clothes."

"I know." He grinned sheepishly. "I started doing it at first through my clothes too."

"I guess it feels like less of a sin that way." I grinned back. "Oh, Eli, it can't be a sin…it feels so very good."

"I know." He swallowed hard, still watching, his hand moving to undo his breeches and reach inside. I wanted to see him too. "Sarah…" His hand reached out, hesitated. "Can I… can I touch it?"

"Can I?" My eyes dropped to where his hand was wrapped around his privates.

He startled. "Do you want to?"

I nodded, my hand out, tentative. He moved forward so I could reach, gasping when I brushed the tip with my fingers. It was a little wet there, and I rubbed that over the top, making him moan.

"Oh that's so nice." He groaned as I wrapped my hand around it like I'd seen him do. It was thick and pulsing, and not anything like I'd expected. I explored for a moment, curious, until I felt his fingers parting me down there, slipping through the wetness.

"Oh, Eli!" I breathed, my legs parting themselves as he explored too. It was different when he touched me, and my breath came faster. I squeezed him, tugging, making him jerk and thrust. I liked the motion.

"Rub it here," I said, showing him the spot, and his fingers moved there, making me spread wide and thrust too. It seemed like the natural thing to do.

"I want to see you," he whispered, not asking, just unfastening my clothes, my skirt, my blouse, and I let him. The air was cold, and he stared down at me, completely

nude before him, no longer seeing me with a brother's eyes. "Oh Sarah, you're the most beautiful thing I've ever seen."

I glowed from the inside out, and when he leaned in and took one of my nipples into his mouth, the way I'd seen the babies do, latching on to Ma for milk, I thought the sensation would make me faint.

"More," I whispered, my hand in his hair, arching my back. "Suck them hard."

He groaned, burying his face there, licking and sucking, his privates swelling even larger in my hand. My whole body was on fire, his fingers probing between my legs, finding a place I had never explored and slipping inside.

"Eli!" I gasped when another entered me. He was inside—his fingers were *inside* of me.

"It's how men and women join together," he whispered against my neck, fingers moving, in and out. "It feels... it's..."

"Oh Eli," I moaned, rocking, tugging at him, aching for more of everything all at once. "Please, yes, please, let's..."

He moved on top of me and I took the weight of him, the long length of his privates rubbing up against mine as we kissed. His mouth was hot, urgent, his hands buried in the length of my hair, completely down now and spread out on the hay beneath us. He rocked on top of me, rubbing the tender spot until I thought I would die, kissing my breasts, sucking my nipples, sending me flying.

"Eli, oh, oh, it's happening," I whispered, closing my eyes as my body took flight, shuddering involuntarily underneath him. His breath was hot in my ear as he whispered my name, shifting his hips and pressing hard. I gasped, clinging to him as he entered me, feeling my body opening to him in a bright red burst.

"Ooooooooohhh!" he gasped, shivering, and I pulled him to me, the hot throb of him between my legs almost too much to bear. "Sarah, Sarah, oh you feel so good."

"Yes," I whispered as he rocked, thrust, shuddered. I kissed his cheeks, his chin, his neck, as he moved deeper,

faster, until he gave a great, sudden cry and collapsed in my arms, trembling with the force of the explosion inside of him.

We held each other close in the hazy afternoon light coming through the slats in the barn, stunned by each other, by the world, by everything we had ever thought or believed was true.

"It's not a sin," I whispered, stroking his sweat-dampened hair.

"No." He shook his head and kissed me breathless until everything faded away. Finally, nothing else mattered but me and Eli and the weight of the world was lifted.

Under the Stars (Sibling Lust)

"I don't know what you see in him anyway." Sam was sarcastically trying to cheer me up about my boyfriend cancelling at the last minute, but I was ready to hit my brother over the head with the tent pole he was carrying in from the car. "If Jake went to a mind-reader, they'd only charge him half price."

"Shut up, Sam." I continued unpacking all our food 'staples'—flour, rice, canned soup, boxed macaroni and cheese—slamming them on the counter. I was in no mood, glaring at my brother as he made another trip back out to the car, practically yelling so he could hear me. "What about Erin? You want to bet she wasn't really sick—she just wanted to go to Chicago with Dan!"

"Yow." My brother chucked our sleeping bags onto the floor of the cabin as he came back in, red-faced from exertion or anger, I wasn't sure which—and I didn't care. "You get up on the wrong side of the cage this morning or what?"

"Ugh!" I threw up my hands, reaching for my bottled water and waving him away. "Sam, why don't you just wander outside, like the two-year-old you are, and go play hide-and-fuck-yourself!"

"Ooo, burn." He rolled his eyes, tossing the last of our stuff from the car onto the floor. "Look, I didn't just spend nine hours in a car with you so we could fight all weekend."

"Save your breath." I took a swig of water. "You're going to need it to inflate your new girlfriend."

"Look who's talking?" He snorted, shoving our piles of stuff further into the cabin with his foot so he could slam the door behind him. "At least my girlfriend had a reasonable excuse. What was Jake's?"

I blinked fast, turning away from him and unpacking grocery bags, saying in a small voice, "He said he had to work."

"Right. Sure he did." Sam grabbed his own backpack and slung it over his shoulder, carrying it down the hallway to the room he would have shared with Erin, calling back over his shoulder, "Can't bait a hook, can't pitch a tent. What did you think he was going to do up here anyway?"

I gave up on the groceries, folding my arms and turning to look out the window over the sink. There was nothing to see except miles and miles of state land out back, with the shore of Ontonagon's Thunder Bay to the right. It was quiet, serene, beautiful—and I'd never felt more alone in my life.

"Keep me company." I answered Sam's question, too soft for him to hear, my eyes filling with tears as I remembered Jake's promise saying he would accompany me to the great outdoors in spite of his misgivings. He was definitely more of an inside kind of guy, to be sure. But that didn't mean we couldn't have had fun. He'd bailed on me at the last minute and now I was stuck here alone with my brother instead.

"Hey Sissy." Sam's presence behind me made me stiffen at first, then I relaxed as he put his arms around me, giving me a squeeze. Sissy wasn't my real name, but it's what everyone had called me since my parents adopted Sam when he was just two and couldn't say my name—Cecilia. "I'll keep you company."

"Did you just swallow a happy pill?" I retorted, but I put my hands over his at my waist, taking a deep, relaxing breath, watching the wind sway the trees, the leaves shifting

in the wind, back and forth, like schools of silver minnows. It couldn't have been a more beautiful day.

"I said I didn't want to fight with you, didn't I?" Sam's hands moved to my hips, his fingers starting their precarious trip up my rib cage. I refused to even giggle, although I did smile—I was incredibly ticklish and holding back took a lot of energy.

I twisted away from him before I started to laugh, trying to hang onto my anger. "Could've fooled me."

Sam raised an eyebrow, his mouth twisting into a knowing smirk. We were adopted siblings, from two different families, but our coloring was quite similar—dark hair and eyes. Our adopted mother—the only mother either of us had ever known—had remarked on our striking similarities our whole lives, pleased both of her children not only looked like each other, but like her as well.

My brother grabbed the edge of his t-shirt, pulling over his head and tossing it on the counter, revealing a broad, tanned chest and washboard abs. He'd been working out! "Come on, let's go cool off. It's too fucking hot in here."

He was right. The cabin had been closed up all summer and it was stuffy—far too hot and musty.

I grinned, grabbing the edge of my t-shirt and pulling it over my head too. "Race you!"

Sam gaped at me in my bra, which gave me a good head start as I streaked past him, pulling the door open and pounding down the front porch steps.

"Brat!" my brother called, trailing behind me as I dashed down the path toward the water. Lake Superior was the coldest of the Great Lakes but we had swum in it a hundred times during hot August vacations like this one with our parents. This time, since Mom and Dad had decided to go on a long-awaited trip to Europe, Sam and I had finally been allowed to come up here by ourselves.

I already had my shorts undone, shoving them down my hips as I reached the water's edge, kicking off my flip-flops. I left my panties on—they covered more than my bikini

would have anyway—and splashed into the lake, screeching at the cold, but Sam was after me.

"Cold!" I warned over my shoulder—as if he couldn't have figured that out by my initial reaction—seeing him stripping down to his boxers.

I plunged in up to my neck, shivering, knowing the sooner I went under, the better my body would acclimate to the temperature. The water was a deep, dark blue, the wind high, creating white crests all around me as I held my breath and slipped below the surface. The world went away and I reveled in the sensation, staying down as long as I could, until my lungs began to ache.

That's when Sam caught up to me, grabbing me around the waist from behind and swimming with me to the top. I drew a big breath as we surfaced and squealed as he tossed me into the waves. I came up sputtering, laughing, splashing my brother as I tried to swim away.

"Don't go out too far," he warned, giving up the chase and floating on his back, letting the waves rock him. I did the same, the sun warm on my face, for the first time really glad we'd come, in spite of the fact it was under less-than-perfect circumstances. So Jake had chickened out—I didn't need him to enjoy the weekend. And Sam didn't need Erin. We could make do, hanging out together like this, as long as we could keep from fighting!

As if to prove me wrong, I felt a sudden, sharp poke on my thigh and I jumped, gasping.

"Sam!" I protested, uprighting myself and treading water, but he was too far away to have touched me, still lazily floating.

"What?" he called, popping up too, shading his eyes to look over at me.

I rubbed my leg, frowning. "I thought you pinched me!"

"Must have been a fish." He laughed. "Come on, let's go in. I'm getting hungry. Tomorrow we'll catch the little bastard and eat him."

I followed him toward shore, shivering when the air hit my skin as we waded out. I saw Sam glance at me in my bra and panties and I looked down, realizing my white underwear was now completely see-through.

"Too bad Jake isn't here." He grinned, tossing my clothes at me. "He'd enjoy the show."

We ate dinner on the porch—Beef Sirloin Chunky soup warmed up on the stove—sitting in the orange glow of the sun setting over the lake. It was peaceful and quiet, and Sam and I caught up on what had been going on at school this year. I had just finished my first year of college at Michigan State. Sam teased me about going to "farm school." He'd been at the University of Michigan for two years on a full scholarship. We both stayed clear of the subject of my missing boyfriend and his "sick" girlfriend.

"Tired," I announced finally, looking up at the stars studding the night, like hundreds of tiny jewels on black velvet. "I'm gonna go to bed."

"Night, Sissy." I couldn't see his smile in the darkness, but I could hear it. "Sleep tight, don't let the bedbugs bite."

The phrase from childhood made me smile as I cleared our soup bowls, leaving them in the sink before heading to the room I would have shared with Jake. But I didn't want to think about him, I told myself, checking my cell phone for messages anyway. There were none.

I stripped down to nothing—*which I definitely would have done if Jake was here,* I thought, with a touch of regret—and slid between the cool, clean sheets I'd put on the bed. I left my window open so I could hear the light chirp of crickets and the deeper call of the bullfrogs. Besides, it was still warm, my hair sticking to the moist skin of my shoulders and back.

I'd imagined the perfect, romantic weekend getaway, Jake and I tucked away at night in this bed, kissing and touching and trying to be quiet so my brother and Erin didn't know what we were doing in here. My mind tried to argue I didn't miss him, but my body knew better. Sighing, I

closed my eyes, sliding my hand down between my legs. My pussy was throbbing, in need of attention, and I decided to give it some, since Jake wasn't here to do it.

My fingers slipped between my pussy lips, teasing my clit, imagining how sweet Jake's tongue was right there—when I could get him to stay there long enough to make me come, anyway. I mimicked his usual motion with my finger, back and forth, up and down. I tugged and pulled at my nipples with my other hand, my breath coming faster, my hips thrusting up, the sheet falling away. Soon I was so lost in the sensation I forgot everything else.

"Hey Sissy?" Sam knocked, but he opened the door right after, poking his head in. I gasped, grabbing for the sheet, pulling it up to my neck, praying he hadn't seen anything, telling myself surely, *surely* it was too dark for his eyes to have adjusted so quickly!

"What?" I snapped, feeling my face flush with heat, glad for the darkness.

"Um…" He hesitated in the doorway while I inwardly squirmed.

He didn't see anything!
Maybe he did.
He didn't!
What if he did?!

Sam cleared his throat. "I just wanted to know if you wanted to go with me tomorrow."

I bit my lip, my fingers sticky wet against my belly. "Go where?"

"I wanted to take the tent out to the ridge tomorrow," he explained. "The salmon are running early."

"Okay," I squeaked, mostly just to get him to shut the door.

"Goodnight, Sissy." His voice was warm. What had he seen? Oh god.

"'Night, Sam."

I let out a breath, hearing his footfalls down the hallway, his door closing behind him.

I probably should have been completely turned off, considering what had just happened, but the opposite was strangely true. I was even more excited, my body humming and tingling, my little clit thrumming, and I strummed it like a guitar with too-tight strings ready to snap.

"Oh yes," I whispered, my legs parting, the sound of my fingers rubbing through my wetness filling the room. I was going to come—so hard, so very hard! My eyes closed in the darkness and the image that filled my inner vision was my brother, Sam, standing there without his shirt on, grinning at me. Oh god, no. No, no, no. I tried to change the channel in my brain, to think of anything, anyone else, but it was no use.

"Sam," I moaned, I couldn't help it, shaking my head against the mattress, the fullness between my legs too much to bear. "Ohhhh!"

The world exploded, my limbs trembling with the force of my orgasm, my mouth open in a silent scream. I gasped and quivered on the bed, rolling myself up in the coolness of the sheet, looking for some comfort now, still ashamed of where my mind had gone, unbidden. There was nothing there but my pillow, so I hugged it fiercely, closing my eyes and searching hard for sleep.

I finally found it, the sound of the waves against the shore rocking me there like a lullaby.

* * * *

It was far too hot, as far as I was concerned, to do much but soak in the sun, but I'd agree to hike out to the ridge with Sam before the sun even rose over the lake so he could go fly-fishing in the shallows. I made him set up the tent, though, so I could crawl in and sleep until ten or so, brewing coffee over the fire when I woke and changing into my bikini by noon, so I could spread a blanket on the sand and sleep again.

I rolled over to my belly, feeling sweat sliding down my sides, and grabbed the baby oil, rubbing it, slick and greasy, over my already tanned skin. I shaded my eyes and saw Sam

out there in his hip-boots, no shirt on, casting a line, and couldn't help but thinking of the night before. I flushed, grateful for the heat of the sun.

Then I saw him glance over at me. He saw me watching him.

"Catch anything?" I called.

He just waved and went back to fishing.

What did he see last night? I wondered.

It made me remember the time I'd walked in on him when we were younger. He'd found one of Dad's porno mags and was wanking away in the bathroom, the thing unfurled onto the counter, his nose almost touching the pink of the girl's spread-open pussy. When I opened the door and he stood, dick still in hand, it was the first time I'd seen a real erect cock. It looked huge to me, all shiny and covered in oil—there had been a bottle of baby oil on the counter.

Just the smell of the stuff, and the smooth feel of it on my skin, made me remember.

"Fuck!" he'd cried, reaching for the door and closing it again. "Knock, would you?"

"Maybe you should try locking it!" I'd called back, disgusted—but I had to admit, I was curious too. His room was next to mine for years, and sometimes I heard the distinct sound of him masturbating. The oil wasn't just a bathroom thing, because I could hear the slick sound of his hand moving up and down, the muffled cries of his climax.

I couldn't deny it had turned me on. I knew it wasn't supposed to—I should have been disgusted, horrified, sickened. But I wasn't. Watching Sam, hearing him come, had made me curious. The first time I'd ever orgasmed, I'd been listening to Sam jerk off in his room.

"You know how to gut a fish?"

I lifted my sunglasses as Sam dropped a bucket into the sand next to me.

"You caught something!" I sat up to peer in at a stillgaping salmon, its staring eye not yet filmy. "Ugh! You want me to clean it?"

Sam was stripping off his waders and I couldn't help watching. "You should do something to contribute besides lying around half naked."

I raised my eyebrows at him as he left his pole and rod and reel in the sand, heading down the shoreline in just his jeans and tennis shoes.

"Where are you going?" I called.

"Downstream. I need to wash off." The water here was far too shallow to really bathe in. "Clean the damned fish!"

I watched him until he disappeared around a bend, where I couldn't see any more through a cluster of trees. I turned my attention to the fish—fresh caught salmon was going to be so yummy!—but I didn't feel like getting my hands dirty.

Instead, I followed Sam. I needed to wash off, too, considering how covered I was in oil. That's what I told myself as I rounded the bend to find my brother naked in the water, his hand wrapped around his hard cock, fist pumping furiously. His eyes were closed tight, so he didn't see me stop short and slide behind one of the trees so I could continue to watch him. We hadn't seen any other campers, but I wondered at his boldness. What if a boat came by and someone saw? He must have been desperate, I realized, biting my own lip as I watched Sam bite his, my own hips thrusting forward against the biting bark of the tree in time with his own.

"Oh fuck!" I heard him cry, pumping faster, his balls slapping the water with each tug of his cock. "Yeah! Yeahhhh!"

I moaned softly, leaning my cheek against the rough bark, knowing I shouldn't, but I couldn't help myself, my fingers finding their own way into my bikini bottoms. My pussy was wet with my juices, but the baby oil I'd used on my thighs made it even slicker and I sighed with pleasure, rubbing the stuff into my little clit as I watched my brother jerk off.

Cecilia Marie Roberts, you march right back to camp this instant and clean that fish!

Fuck that, I argued with the voice in my head, my fingers rubbing furiously, my nipples hard and poking out against the tree. I was practically fucking the thing, wishing for something hard to rub against, or better yet, put inside me.

Like Sam's cock.

The thought shocked me into orgasm and I bit my lip to keep from crying out. I didn't want Sam to hear me as my body shook and trembled, my knees giving out as I sank to the sandy ground. Sam didn't have those inhibitions though—he was far enough from camp to believe I couldn't hear him. He groaned and pumped and thrust into his own fist, crying out, "Ohhh fuck, your pussy is so good! Ahhh! Ahhh I'm gonna come in your fucking cunt! Ohhhh Sissy! Sissyyyyyy!"

I yelped like a wounded puppy or a surprised kitten, my fingers still caught under the waistband of my bikini, still working my clit, and fuck if I didn't come again, right there on the ground as my brother called my name, imagining himself fucking me. Oh god, yes, the thought of his hard dick pummeling my flesh, feeling him explode inside of me, that was more than enough to send me over the edge one more time.

He was thinking about me.

The realization made me shake all over as I watched him recover from his orgasm, his head down, his cock going slowly limp in his hand. And then I crept away, practically running back down the beach, deciding immediately to be a good girl and clean the fish, like I was supposed to be doing all along.

By the time Sam came whistling back around the corner, smiling and waving to me, the salmon was ready to be cooked. It was hard to look into his eyes, so I didn't, telling him I wanted to go down and wash up too.

"But I'm hungry!" he protested.

"I'm all sticky and hot and full of oil," I reminded him, but he didn't need a reminder. I saw it out of the corner of my eye, the way he looked at me in my red and white polka dot bikini. He was hungry all right, but I wasn't sure it was for food.

"I'll make dinner then," he grumbled as I headed down the beach.

I didn't touch myself, like Sam had, although I couldn't help thinking about it. Instead, I washed the oil from my skin and hair with ecologically-sound soap, shaking myself off and putting on a t-shirt and a pair of silky shorts. By the time I got back to where we were camped, Sam had cooked the salmon but four ears of corn we'd brought along from the cabin.

"That smells divine!" I sat beside him, taking the plate he offered. We ate with our fingers, the fish fresh and flaky, absolutely perfect. We ate our corn noisily, no butter or salt, laughing at the errant kernels that ended up on our faces or even more bellies.

I did my girl-duty and cleaned up while Sam relaxed on the beach, an arm thrown over his eyes. The sun was setting over the water on our second—and last—day of our weekend. Tomorrow was Sunday, and we'd be heading back home. We both had reasons to be back. Sam had work at our local hardware store Monday afternoon, and I had a dentist appointment.

My brother woke as I sat down beside him on the blanket. We were quiet as we watched the stars come out one by one, the moon a mere sliver as it rose slowly until it was high overhead. We didn't talk, we just sat, comfortable in the silence, until I started to shiver. The breeze off the lake was growing cool.

"Cold?" Sam slid closer, putting an arm around me.

I leaned my head against his shoulder, taking comfort in his warmth. "I'm glad we came."

"Me too." He took a deep, slow breath, gathering the blanket up so he could wrap that around us both. "I'm going to miss you."

"I know." We'd been home together all summer break, but it was August and soon it would be time to go back to school again. It was funny, but I thought I might miss Sam more than I was going to miss Jake. None of us went to the same college, although Jake kept talking about transferring to State, and long-distance relationships weren't easy.

"Hey, look." Sam pointed over the lake and I gasped, seeing a faint haze of multi-colored lights swirling in the sky.

"Is that what I think it is?"

Sam nodded. "Northern lights."

"Beautiful," I breathed

"Yes." I felt his lips brush my temple and I shivered.

"Still cold?"

"A little," I lied. "I think I'm gonna go to bed."

"Okay." He sounded a little disappointed, but I couldn't trust myself, so close to him like this. It was far too dangerous. "I'll wait and put out the fire."

I stood, heading for our tent, calling over my shoulder. "G'night, Sam."

"G'night, Sissy," he said softly as I unzipped the tent and climbed in.

I took off my shorts and crawled into my sleeping bag, sure I wasn't going to be able to sleep right away, if at all, but I was wrong.

* * * *

I wasn't sure what woke me. I was disoriented, unsure where I was, until I heard the sound of the waves against the shore. It was still full-dark, very late—or very early. Behind me, Sam was asleep, breathing deeply. Then I felt what had woken me as my brother groaned and shifted again—I felt his erection against my lower back and gasped, the heat of it incredible, even through his boxers.

"Sam?" I whispered, feeling the roll of his hips forward, wedging his cock against the crack of my ass. I was wearing a t-shirt and panties, but things had gotten all twisted while we slept, and my sleeping bag was somewhere down near my ankles.

"Mmm no more," he mumbled. "There are plain ones on the counter."

I blinked in the darkness, trying to decipher this code. The feel of his cock against my ass made me ache. I try to wiggle away, but his hand was on my hip and I couldn't escape. Was he asleep or awake?

"I want one," he whispered, close to my ear. "Gimme."

"Sam, are you sleeping?"

He moaned softly and his hips began to move, the shaft of his erection rubbing slowly, bunching my panties up between my ass cheeks. I felt the grip of his fingers on my hip, my ass, heard his breath coming faster. Was he really still sleeping? I glanced over my shoulder to see, but it was too dark to tell if his eyes were open or closed.

"Sam?" I whispered again, a little louder. Maybe I could wake him up? *Should* I wake him up? Wasn't waking up sleepwalking people dangerous or something? I remembered when we were kids, he used to sleepwalk all the time. My parents would find him in the kitchen or trying to get out the back door. They used to just guide him back to bed, and he never remembered anything in the morning.

"Mmmmm." Sam moaned again and this time the thrust of his hips was more violent. Oh my god, his cock was free! How had that happened? I whimpered, feeling the hard press of him against my ass, the head slick against my lower back, sliding easily. It would just take a little maneuvering, nudging my panties aside, a shift of my hips, and he could be inside me.

He's your brother!

I gasped as Sam moved, his hips adjusting, his cock too, oh god, now he *was* pressed between my thighs, his shaft rubbing between them. My pussy felt fat and hot. I

- 44 -

whimpered again, trying once more to wiggle away, but it only forced him further between my legs, his cock wedging my panties deep between my swollen pussy lips.

"Sam," I moaned as he began to thrust in his sleep, driving my panties through my slick slit, the head of his cock rubbing against my clit. I spread my legs more for him. I couldn't help it. Oh that was good. So fucking good.

This isn't happening. That's what I told myself as I arched back against him. *I'm dreaming.*

I found my hand between my own legs, pulling my sticky-wet panties aside so I could feel the head of his dick rubbing against my clit. But I wanted more. Oh god, what was wrong with me?

"Sam?" I asked, louder this time. He didn't answer me. Instead, he groaned and grunted and thrust. He was sleeping, I was sure of it. He wouldn't remember any of this in the morning.

I pressed his cockhead against my clit with my fingers, rubbing it there, moaning and arching back. My pussy lips wrapped themselves around his shaft, almost like we were fucking, but it still wasn't enough. I took him in my hand, marveling at the heat and thrust of him. So big!

I wanted it. I wanted him.

I aimed carefully, timing it to match his mindless thrusting, and found myself impaled with the next forward movement of his hips, both of us moaning in pleasure, Sam in his sleep, me fully aware of the wicked, horrible thing I'd just done.

But it felt so fucking *good!*

"Oh god," I cried, trying not to move, trying not to rock back, imagining his horrified reaction if he woke up and realized he was fucking his sister!

But he was already imagining it out by the lake.

Had he really been fantasizing about fucking me while he jerked off? He'd called my name as he came, I remembered, flushing with the memory of how hard I'd climaxed just watching him.

"Ahhhh! Ahhhh!" He was thrusting hard and deep and fast. I was going to have to work to keep up, I realized, my fingers slippery wet, finding my clit and rubbing furiously. Oh but it wasn't going to take long, I could tell. My pussy was already beginning to spasm around his shaft. I could feel how deep he was inside, the head of him buried in me.

"Oh no! Oh god!" I cried out, nearly sobbing with the reality of what we were doing, but I still couldn't help myself. It felt too good, too right, my pussy aching for release. And it was coming. I was going to climax around my brother's cock.

Sam's fingers dug deep into my hips as he thrust again, his breath hot against my neck, and I buried my face in my pillow to keep him from hearing my scream as he drove me to my own orgasm, my pussy clamping down around his shaft, snapping shut again and again on his length. I felt each pulse of his dick, felt his cum, not inside of me but seeping out, as if he'd come so much I couldn't contain it all.

I sobbed into my pillow, overwhelmed with emotion, devastated by what I'd done, too limp and shocked to move, but when Sam sighed and moaned in his sleep, sliding his arm up to my waist, his face buried in my hair, I slowly began to relax.

"Sam?" I whispered into the darkness. "Are you sleeping?"

No answer. I reached down and covered myself with my sleeping bag, hoping to cover up what we'd done. It wasn't right, I shouldn't have done it, I knew that. But it would be okay. He would wake in the morning with no memory of it. That's what I told myself as I drifted off to sleep listening to the soft sound of rain starting to fall.

* * * *

"Sissy."

I heard him saying my name, felt his lips, feathery light, over my neck. Then his hands, moving up my hip, under my

shirt. His hand cupped my breast and I gasped, my eyes flying open wide.

"Sam!"

"Shhhh." His cock was hard, still between my legs. *Oh god, it wasn't a dream.*

I moaned softly as he thumbed my hardening nipple, shaking my head. "No, Sam, no…"

"Yes, Sissy, yes" he whispered, and I felt him throbbing between my thighs. *"Yes."*

It was still raining outside, a soft patter on the roof of the tent. "Sam, we can't."

"We already did." His breath was hot against my ear.

I gasped, turning in his arms. "You weren't sleeping?"

"No." He grinned. "At least, not for all of it."

"Sam." I stroked his cheek with my fingertips. I knew I should have been shocked, appalled. Something else besides—thrilled. But I couldn't help what I felt. "Oh Sam… I love you. I've always loved you."

"I know. Me too."

And then he kissed me, and all was lost. Our bodies had known far before we did what we wanted, no, *needed,* from each other, and we both found it in the most unlikely yet natural place in the world—our sibling's arms.

Darla (Daddy's Favorites)

Two "Rock-a-Bye Babies" and four "Bears Over the Mountain" later, Darla finally tucked her baby sister in and turned out the light. There was a Barney nightlight by her bed that glowed an eerie purple. It was cold outside, snowing lightly, and it was cold in here. Only Carrie's blonde curls, shorter and a shade lighter than Darla's sleek mane, peeked out from above the pink covers.

"Don't let the bedbugs bite," Darla whispered, easing the door closed. That's what her dad had always said to her, when she was around Carrie's age, and it came out of her mouth automatically. It made her suddenly sad.

"Not all the way," Carrie piped up, her voice muffled. Darla left the door open a crack and went to see what her dad had to eat in the kitchen. She was hoping for ice cream and hit pay dirt—a pint of Haagen-Dazs. It was probably Irene's, and Darla took a great deal of pleasure in knowing she might be eating the last of her stepmother's favorite Rum Raisin as she settled in front of a rerun of Friends.

She glanced at the clock when the show was over. Only ten. They said they were going to be gone probably until midnight. She fantasized for a moment about what she was going to do with the babysitting money, doing the math in her head. The longer they stayed out, the more she would get paid. She might finally have enough to get the iPod she wanted. Her mother had told her at Christmas that maybe by her next birthday but February third had just come and gone,

she'd turned eighteen, but no iPod was forthcoming. Of course, her mother blamed it on her father. He had all the money. Why didn't he buy her one of the damned things, her mother wanted to know?

But Darla knew. Her parents had adopted her when she was just a newborn, and she had known only goodness and love for a long time. That was until her adopted father left them for another woman. Now he had a new daughter of his own—his very own. Darla was just an afterthought, something that had happened to him in a former life. She wasn't really his.

Darla sat and looked around the room, which was probably bigger than their living room and kitchen combined. The whole house must have been at least five thousand square feet. She had never even seen the whole thing.

That was something she could do. Time to do some exploring. Carrie's room was down a long hallway which included Darla's room when she stayed over, and a separate bathroom. She had seen all of that. There were several guest rooms, another bathroom, her dad's office, and Irene's scrapbooking room at the back of the house. Upstairs beyond her dad's bedroom, though, she had no idea what was back there.

Their room was spacious and white. Everything was pristine—the rug, the bed, the furniture. She glanced at the bed, which was made but kind of rumpled on one side, as if someone had been sitting there. She reclined on it, gasping at the softness of the down comforter, the sinking of the mattress underneath her. Her eyes closed, and she let herself drift, lost and floating on a cloud in the darkness. She thought she could smell her daddy, his aftershave maybe, lingering on the sheets. When her eyes opened, she gasped again, seeing her reflection staring back at her. There was a mirror over the bed!

She looked at her own stunned expression, her long hair spread out beneath her head over the whiteness of the

comforter like a gossamer river running through drifts of snow. What would you need a mirror on the ceiling for? She looked at her soft belly, exposed now with her arms flung carelessly above her head, a pale, white expanse of skin between her "American Idol" t-shirt and the black miniskirt her mother kept having a fit about her father buying her for Christmas, which she insisted on wearing, even out in the snow. She rubbed her tummy somewhat self-consciously. It was smooth and flat, her navel the only dip in the surface, no other hint of a softening curve.

She lifted her shirt higher, then higher still, never having seen herself from such a vantage point. Her breasts weren't much more than buds, her pink nipples hardening as the cool air moved over them. She was slightly disappointed that they looked even smaller when she was lying down.

She had given up hope she was going to develop something to fill the bras that had been waiting in her drawer since her thirteenth Christmas. Her mother had seen her just beginning to develop and had insisted on buying them, and they had sat there for years, embarrassing her. Other girls got curves, breasts, while Darla watched longingly, hoping for those things for herself.

She wondered at the mirror again. Probably her stepmother, she decided. Had to make sure she looked good, even at night. She hopped off the bed, going to explore the rest of whatever was down this hallway. She glanced in their bathroom, which was right off their bedroom. It was huge too, of course, with a corner Jacuzzi tub surrounded by unlit candles, and there was a separate shower with a showerhead at each end. The mirror and sink and vanity ran the length of one wall. His and hers sinks even. She saw her father's shaving stuff on the counter.

She was about to leave the room to continue her exploration when she glanced in their closet. Her stepmother had expensive tastes. There were dresses galore in the walk-in closet, a whole wall full. She ran her hands lightly over the fabrics—silks and satins and velvets. A shimmery green

dress called out to her, and she plucked it from the hanger. It was short, with a plunging neckline, completely sleeveless, the top of it just two pieces of material that tied behind the neck. The skirt would probably have come to her tall, long-legged stepmother's mid-thigh. Maybe. It was completely backless.

Darla carried it over to the mirror at the end of the closet. It was one of those three way things, like they had in department stores, so you could see yourself at every angle. In the light, it really sparkled, like the dress was made of thousands of iridescent emeralds. She was mesmerized. Suddenly, she was pulling off her t-shirt, unzipping her skirt and sliding it down over her white cotton panties. Considering for a moment, she slid those off too, standing there completely naked. She turned this way and that, admiring her slight figure in the mirror.

She turned, liking the view from behind, it was at least one place she had curves, in the soft rounded cheeks of her bottom. From the side, if she exaggerated and stuck her chest out, she could imagine her breasts were fuller and rounder instead of the barely emerged nodes they really were. She looked at the dress in her hands again, glancing at the tag inside. *Versace*. She slid it up the long length of her thin frame, moving her hair out of the way so she could tie it, gasping at the feel of it against her skin.

She piled her hair up on top of her head, admiring herself. The dress was too long and the front simply hung on her—her nascent breasts did nothing to fill it. When she turned, she giggled, seeing the crack of her butt appearing above the back of the dress. It shimmered deliciously when she moved.

She danced, sylphlike, her reedy arms stretched above her head, swaying willowy, back and forth, pursing her lips, widening her eyes at the mirror. Irene had hundreds of these dresses and she wore them out every weekend. Darla felt suddenly very jealous. Her daddy, who she now only saw a

few times a month at the most, spent hours with the woman who filled these dresses. Who filled *this* dress.

What's he ever given me*?* Darla fingered the heart-shaped locket she'd had since she was little, the one thing her adopted father had left behind. She sometimes imagined she had captured his real heart in it, keeping it like a secret from anyone else. Closing her eyes, she began to dance again, holding her father's heart in her hand.

What would it be like, she wondered, *to have a man hold you, press you against him, kiss you?* She closed her eyes and imagined dancing with a boy—no, a man. She found it was her daddy she was imagining, his large, strong hands guiding her, his eyes bright and full of love as he looked down at her. She was so lost in the fantasy she could even smell his aftershave.

"Kiss me, Daddy," she murmured, her eyes still closed, tilting her head up like she saw in all the movies.

"Darla." The sound of her name made her whirl around and stumble over her discarded clothes. She landed bone-jarringly hard on her bottom and she whimpered, leaning back on her elbows. Her father stood in the doorway, his large frame filling it completely. She felt her whole body flush with embarrassment.

Oh no, oh god, this can't be happening.

They didn't say anything for a moment and Darla found herself trembling. He cleared his throat. "Why don't you get your own clothes back on, sweetheart? I have to take you back to your mother's tonight."

She forgot what she was wearing, what she had been caught doing, she forgot everything at those words. "But... I thought I was going to stay here tonight, Daddy! You said...we were going to go to the movies tomorrow!" She struggled to contain her tears and lost, but at least she did it silently. She swallowed around the hard lump in her throat.

"I know, honey, but Irene isn't feeling well. She's downstairs lying on the couch. I'm glad she didn't come up

here first," he chuckled. "I'll make it up to you, angel. I promise."

She nodded, looking down at his shoes, his dress shoes. They had gone to a play tonight. *Taming of the Shrew*. She didn't want him to see she was crying.

"I'll get dressed," she said, wanting him to go before she really started sobbing. "Be down in a minute."

"Ok…and Darla, honey…don't forget your panties." He turned around, his voice sounding strained.

She snapped her slim thighs closed, her face burning. She had forgotten entirely she wasn't wearing any.

* * * *

Darla put the dress back and hurriedly pulled on her clothes. She stopped in the bathroom to smooth her hair into a ponytail and wash her face, still wet, and gave herself a good talking-to in order to stop the tears. There was no way she was going to go downstairs crying. Now she was putting on her coat, and she smiled, pleased, as her father helped her while she pulled her hair out from under the collar.

"Lee, did you pay her? Darla, thank you for watching your sister," Irene murmured from the couch where she was lying with her arm thrown over her eyes.

"She's not my real sister!" Darla hissed, surprising both of them and herself.

"Money's in your coat pocket, sweetie." Her father looked sideways at her. "And you did a fine job too. I told you she would, Irene."

There was a snort from the couch.

"Come on, let's get going," he said.

She followed him out the door, shouldering her backpack with all her school work and a change of clothes for the weekend she wouldn't be needing anymore. Tears stung her eyes again at the thought. The two-seater Jaguar was still warm from their ride home. Darla turned the radio station first thing. He always let her. She turned it up loud. She didn't want to talk.

When they pulled into the driveway half an hour later, the house was dark and her mother's car was gone. Her father swore under his breath and Darla looked at him sharply. He grabbed his cell phone out of his pocket and flipped it open, hitting the "talk" button. She heard the phone ringing, and the answering machine with her own voice saying, "You've reached the Somers residence. We're not here right now..."

"You didn't call her?" Darla sighed.

"I called her." His mouth was a thin line. "She said she'd be here.

"Figures." Darla shoved the door open and ran up the walkway. She fumbled in her coat pocket for her keys, finding the money her father had left there to pay her for babysitting. It was far more than she'd really earned. She was crying in earnest now, and she tossed the money angrily into the snow. She got the door open, the warmth and familiar smell of home a dubious welcome, shrugging off her jacket and throwing her backpack in the foyer.

"Hey, Darla." Her father peeked his head inside and she turned her back to him, not wanting him to see her puffy eyes. "You dropped this, honey."

"I didn't drop it."

"Isn't this your babysitting money?" His voice was right behind her now. She could feel the chill from the outside he carried with him.

"Yes, but I didn't drop it. I threw it there," she snarled, moving away from him and flopping onto the couch, crossing her arms over her chest and lowering her head to let her hair hide her face.

"Why?" He sounded genuinely confused. She struggled with a response, trying to speak around the tightness in her throat.

How can he not know, how can he not see? "I don't want your money." It was barely a whisper.

"What was that, sweetie?" He was sitting next to her on the couch, moving to brush her hair away from her face.

She jerked away. "I don't want your money!" She shoved at him and moved to stand. She was off balance and he grabbed her arm to help steady her.

"Hey, hey." He held both of her wrists now as she struggled to get away. "Come here." He pulled her toward him and although she resisted at first, she finally relented and let him settle her onto his lap.

She repeated it over and over under her breath, like a mantra to keep her from breaking down entirely. "I don't want your money."

"Okay, okay," he murmured. "What *do* you want, honey?"

"You!" she wailed, leaning into him and putting her arms around his neck. "You're all I've ever wanted, Daddy. I never wanted anything else." She feathered little kisses on his throat and collarbone, rubbing the smooth skin of her cheek against the whiskers on his chin.

"Oh, angel," he whispered into her hair, stroking her back. "You have me. You've always had me."

She was trying to get as close as she possibly could, wrapping her bare legs around him. He helped her, unbuttoning his coat so she could sidle closer, enveloping her in his arms.

"I'm so sorry it's turned out this way, sweetheart. I never meant—" His voice was hoarse, pained.

"Hold me, Daddy," she whispered, pressing her cheek to his. He did, rocking her gently, stroking her hair. "I miss you so much, you don't know...it makes me hurt all over." She wiggled in his lap and she heard him gasp and let out a small groan. His face was buried in her hair.

"Sweetie, maybe we better—" he started, but she lifted her face suddenly and kissed him just like she had fantasized about in front of the mirror earlier that night.

It wasn't a sweet innocent little girl kiss, it was a real kiss, the way she imagined kissing Tommy Keys who sat behind her in math, the way she imagined kissing Simon

Tina (Daddy's Favorites)

Cacomorphobia.

Tina had texted the question to the instant-answer site *Cha-Cha* on the Internet and they came back right away with the response. Yes, there was a technical name for someone who was afraid of either becoming fat, or afraid of being around fat people. In fact, it was the same word.

She was cacomorphobic. Her political science teacher made them cover current events every week, and Tina always brought in articles about diet, health, nutrition. The latest article she'd shared with the class claimed a new study showed girls were more afraid of being fat than they were of cancer, nuclear war, or losing their parents.

As far as she knew, it was true. It was definitely true for her.

Hell, cancer would be great. Didn't it make you lose weight? As for her parents, her dad was already gone. She lived with her mother—who was also cacomorphobic, but who also happened to be pencil-slim—and her stepfather. If she could trade her parents for being thin, would she? In a heartbeat. Well, at least her mother.

And then there was nuclear war—the ultimate weight-loss solution.

Tina stood nude after her shower, hands on hips, looking into the beautifully carved, wooden full-length mirror her mother had set up as "incentive" in the corner of her room. She was fat, there was no doubt about it.

Her hips were rounded, not straight and slim like her mother's. Why, oh why, had she gotten her father's chubby genes? Her lower belly was distended, protruding. Her thighs weren't thighs, they were more like the thick flanks of a horse. And her bottom?

She twisted a quarter-turn, staring at the rounded-bubble swell of her ass. Just like that old song—*baby got back!* And her breasts! Why couldn't she have tiny, perfect, hard little plums? No, she had to have fat, ripe cantaloupes.

Tina twisted back and forth, surveying, wishing she could trade her body in for another model, one that could wear bikinis and mini-skirts and little white tank tops. She just wanted to be one of those girls who bought tiny little bras with the hooks up front instead of a fat row of three in the back.

The funny thing was, if she closed her eyes, her experience of her body was very different than when she was standing in front of the mirror. She liked her curves in the dark, the way her belly dipped at her navel and rose again, a little hill, before the edge of her pubic hair. Her skin was smooth and soft, especially on her thighs, which were well-muscled from years of playing soccer.

Why was it so pleasing to the touch, but so unappealing to the eye?

She closed her eyes, remembering how Ray had put his hands up her shirt in the backseat of his Jeep, the windows as steamy as a shower mirror, squeezing and kneading her breasts like bread dough. The boys had been fascinated with her breasts since sixth grade, when they first started to bud. Ray, her first real boyfriend, had been no exception.

But while Ray was happy to feel her up in the backseat or in her parents' basement, he wasn't so keen on taking her to the movies or out to dinner. When she'd accused him of not wanting to be seen with her, he denied it—but then senior prom came around and he took Susan McNaughton instead, confirming what she'd suspected.

And if there'd been any doubt, the conversation she overheard in the girls' bathroom cinched it. When Susan McNaughton told Liz O'Neal that Ray was taking her to prom, she said, "I heard he was going out with Tina Vale?" Susan had laughed and replied, "That heifer? Please. He'd have to rent a crane!" They had cackled together about it while Tina hid, red-faced, in the bathroom stall.

She thought college would be better, but so far the boys had been the same—they liked to stare at her tits, but the girls who got asked out were the ones who wore skinny jeans and halter tops.

She was ashamed of her own fantasies, of finding a boy who would take her out to dinner and compliment her on her hair and how she looked in her dress, who was proud to have her on his arm. It was true—she wanted to be eye candy.

She kept her eyes closed, letting her hands move over the soft slope of her belly, up her ribs. Her breasts were very heavy in her hands, her coffee-colored nipples sensitive. Luann, her best friend and extremely flat-chested, had once told her girls with large breasts didn't have as sensitive nipples as girls with little ones, but their health teacher had dispelled that myth. Thank goodness they'd been allowed to submit anonymous questions in the suggestion box!

Her nipples were super-sensitive. She'd even made herself climax that way before, and Ray used to make her come just from sucking on them. She could suck her own if she wanted to. When she'd told him that, he'd made her prove it and she had. Smiling at the memory, she lifted her breast to her mouth, sticking her tongue out to lick it. God, that was good. She felt right between her legs.

She rolled her fat nipple between thumb and forefinger, letting her other hand drift slowly down between her thighs. Her pubic hair was dark and curly and she parted her labia with her fingers, finding the hooded little button of her clit. How could something so small make her feel so good?

She bit her lip, circling it—far too sensitive to touch it directly, not yet—feeling her breath coming faster, her nipples growing harder, the skin around them pursed. It made her breathless, wobbly, like her legs wouldn't hold her.

Better—safer—to do this in bed, she decided, opening her eyes and trying to avoid her flushed-cheek reflection in the mirror, water beading on her shoulders from her wet tangle of hair.

That's when she saw him standing in her doorway, his hand still on the knob, eyes wide and glassy, mouth agape.

"Christina," he managed, choking the word out. The look in his eyes was like nothing she'd ever seen, his gaze sweeping her body as she bent to retrieve her towel, realizing too late that she'd just given him quite a view of her behind. "I was… looking…"

"Daddy!" She whirled around and held the towel in front of her, covering her breasts and belly. It fell only to the top of her thighs. "You're supposed to be at work!"

"I was…" He blinked, looking past her now, his eyes avoiding hers. He was dressed for work in a suit and tie, tall and handsome. She'd heard the girls in his office call him "Mr. Hot Lawyer" and his mother complained they all shamelessly flirted with him. "I had to get… I thought you might have seen the…"

"The what?" she squeaked, too embarrassed and humiliated to say more. Her blood was still coursing, hot through her veins, her pussy wet and throbbing from her touch, but her pulse had done nothing but increase since he'd opened her door and surprised her.

"Never mind." He shook his head, looking dazed, his gaze still focused somewhere behind her. There was a dark look in his eyes, like an animal stalking prey, and it made her feel like blushing.

Tina glanced over her shoulder and flushed, realizing the mirror revealed her completely naked from behind. When she turned and met his eyes, the look had intensified.

"I'm sorry," he apologized hoarsely. "Never mind."

"Daddy—" she whispered, but he left, shutting the door behind him.

* * * *

Thank god for Dropbox. She'd had a major disaster senior year when her English Lit term paper disappeared off her hard drive, and now she always, always saved her work somewhere in the cloud. Her stepfather's laptop was going to have to do—her own was locked in Luann's car, forgotten in the back seat, and Luann was out on a date. There was no way to get it back in time, and her French essay was due in the morning.

Tina opened her stepfather's Dell, waiting for the welcome screen to pop up. Her parents were due home any time—they'd gone to some charity thing her mother was involved with—but she knew her stepfather wouldn't mind if she used his computer. She'd done it before.

The screen that appeared surprised her. *Password protected? Since when?* Frustrated, Tina tapped her fingernails on the desk, trying to remember what they had used to lock all the "adult" channels on the television. She and Luann had figured it out—twice—just to see if they could. At first it was their address. Then it was her stepfather's birthdate.

She typed in her stepfather's birthdate. No luck. 1234? No. Her mother's birthday? No. *Damnit.* She could be here doing this all night! *My birthday?* She typed it in and the screen unlocked. Success!

If the password screen had surprised her, what came up next utterly shocked her. There was a video open, with the title, "BBW Gets It Good." *BBW? What's that?* The image was stilled, but it was clear what it was—a heavyset girl with dark hair and eyes, reclining on a bed with her legs spread, her breasts cupped in her hands, while a guy with a very hard cock knelt between them.

"What the hell?" she whispered, licking her lips and leaning in to get a closer look. She knew her stepfather

watched porn—that's why the adult pay channels had been locked—but not *this* kind of porn. The girl on the screen wasn't the usual dyed-blond porn-type with long, tanned legs and fake breasts and a tiny waist. This was a *real* girl, about her age, she guessed—thick and curvy. Her breasts were definitely real. She could tell.

Tina clicked the little triangle in the middle of the screen to make the video play. The sound was off, but she watched as the guy parted the girl's chubby thighs, her pussy shaved smooth, her lips swollen, red and fat as he smacked them with the head of his cock. The girl's head went back as he slid his cock home. She reached for him, and her breasts began to sway as he fucked her. *Yep, definitely real,* Tina noted.

She found the sound and turned it up, frowning when nothing came out of the speakers. Then she noticed the ear buds on her stepfather's big, antique desk, plugged into the laptop. She slipped them into her ears, the sound of fucking filling her head, sending a hot jolt of excitement down between her legs. She followed the sensation with her hand, cupping her mound, rubbing it over her panties—she was wearing just those and a t-shirt, ready for bed—as she watched the girl on the screen get pounded.

She looks like me. She did—at least a little. Definitely her body type, and even her coloring.

"Ohhhh Daddy, yes, fuck your little girl's tight baby pussy!"

Tina gaped at the screen, her breath caught in her throat. Of course, the older man fucking the younger girl on her stepfather's computer wasn't *really* the girl's daddy. That would be illegal. And wrong. But... but somehow the thought that it *might* be, just the fantasy of it, made her pussy ache like it never had before.

Tina leaned back in the big leather chair, putting one foot up on the seat so her legs were spread, rubbing her clit through her panties. Her arousal was so instantaneous, they

were sticky already, the crotch damp as she tugged it aside, letting her fingers play in her wetness.

"You like Daddy's big cock?" the guy on the screen growled, pulling the length of it out so she could see it glistening before driving it back in, deep.

"Yes, Daddy! Oh yes! I love your big fucking dick inside me!" The girl used a kind of sing-song voice, high and sweet, and the man groaned, grabbing onto her breasts as they swayed on her chest. Tina watched as he squeezed and kneaded them, just like Ray used to do to her. Then he rolled her over to her belly, making her get up on her hands and knees.

"Oh god," she whispered, watching as the girl did as she was told, putting her bottom up high, her cheek resting against the mattress. She could almost feel that thick, hard cock sliding into her like that, from behind, those big hands gripping her.

"You've got a gorgeous ass, baby," he groaned, slapping it as he began to pump himself inside her. "Just fucking gorgeous."

Tina flushed at his words, her clit throbbing under her fingers as she rubbed herself, watching the couple on the screen fucking harder, faster, really getting into it now. She was too, so close to coming she was quivering all over. She knew she had to hurry—her parents would be home soon and she didn't want to be caught on her stepfather's password-protected computer. In fact, she was so close, she probably wouldn't have heard it if one of the ear buds hadn't slipped from her ear at that moment.

"I'll be just a few minutes!" her stepfather called on the other side of the door.

Tina just reacted, snapping the computer's lid closed and tossing the ear buds on the desk before sliding underneath it to hide in the cubbyhole. The desk was enormous, antique, so heavy the movers had cursed and grunted getting it up the stairs, and Tina shrank to the very back of the dark space, trying to keep quiet. She was

breathing far too hard, and she gulped, trying to calm her racing heart.

The door opened and she closed her eyes, putting a hand over her own mouth to silence herself. Her stepfather turned on the light—she hadn't bothered—and then locked the door. She heard the tell-tale "click." Tina swallowed, trying to make herself smaller as he came over toward the desk—she heard his dress shoes on the hardwood floor.

She tried not to breathe at all as her stepfather opened his laptop, sitting in the big leather chair where she had just been touching herself. He was still in his suit, and his knees invaded her space as he slid closer to the screen. Oh god—if he found her here...

"There you are, you hot little thing..."

Her eyes widened, sure she was caught, not quite processing the full meaning of his words until he reached under the desk to unzip his fly. *Oh no. Oh my god!* Tina shrank into a ball, hugging her knees, watching as he leaned back in his chair, his cock very erect in his hand. That's when she realized he was watching the same video she'd seen on his computer. Must be!

"Hmmm, let's back this up..." he mused, and she inwardly groaned, knowing the video wasn't at the same place he'd left it. "I want to hear you call me Daddy."

Her eyes widened in surprise, biting her lip and trying not to squirm under the desk as he began to stroke his cock. She couldn't hear the video—he must have the ear buds in, she realized—but she could hear her stepfather's breathing growing heavier, and could see his hand shuttling up and down the length of his cock.

"That's right, baby, Daddy loves your tight little pussy," he whispered, squeezing the head of his dick hard, so hard pre-cum appeared at the tip. Tina bit her lip, watching, fascinated. His cock was nice, fat and long, almost as big as the one in the video. She found herself imagining it in her hand instead of his... in her mouth... in her... *in* her...

Oh no. Her pussy pulsed incessantly between her thighs. *This isn't happening...*

But it was.

"That's right, baby girl, take Daddy's big cock. Oh those fucking tits... that ass... mmmm hell yeah it's gorgeous!"

She remembered that point in the video, when the girl turned over, letting him fuck her from behind. Oh god, she couldn't help herself. Her pussy ached to be touched, and she parted her thighs, letting her hand wander between her legs as quietly as she could. Her stepfather was far too absorbed to notice her, she decided, shivering as her fingers found her sensitive clit. Her pussy was soaking wet!

"Oh fuck, yeah," he whispered, his breath coming so fast, his hand moving even faster, a blur over his cock. "Yeah, yeah, yeah... oh baby girl, I want to fuck that sweet pussy so bad..."

Tina made circles around her clit under the sticky crotch of her panties, trying to keep her breathing under control. She was so close... so very close... and the thought of watching her stepfather ejaculate made her feel dizzy with lust. She licked her lips, daring to lean in a little closer, looking at his balls, hanging over the edge of his zipper, his cockhead almost purple he was so hard.

"Oh baby," he moaned softly. "Tina-baby, my sweet girl, I'm gonna fill you with my cum!"

She had to bite her lip to keep from crying out as she came, her stepfather whispering her name again and again as he shot his cum into his own cupped hand. She watched as the hot, white liquid filled his palm, his hips bucking up toward the top of the desk, her pussy spasming again and again, and she flushed in the darkness, wishing he was inside her, filling her pussy with all his cum, just like he'd said.

"David?" The knock on the door made them both jump, but Tina covered her gasp with her hand, praying her

stepfather was too surprised to notice. "Are you coming to bed?"

"I'll be out in a minute!" he called, standing. She heard him cleaning up, closing the laptop. "I've just got to send one more email!"

Email, yeah right.

"Tina's light's off—I think she's asleep," her mother called. "I'm going to take a bath."

She breathed a silent sigh of relief.

"Okay!" he called. "I'll be right up."

Tina closed her eyes, waiting to be discovered, but her stepfather opened his office door and turned out the light, following her mother down the hall. She waited a long time, as long as she could, sitting in stunned silence in the darkness, still not quite believing what had just happened. Then, she snuck down the hallway, past her parents' closed bedroom door, past the bathroom where the Jacuzzi tub was running, and finally into her own room, hiding herself under the covers and pretending to sleep.

She realized her paper was going to be late, but she didn't care. And it was a long time before she actually slept, tossing and turning, too warm in her own skin to get comfortable. Finally, she did sleep, and she dreamed dreams far too naughty for her to remember when she woke, but they left her feeling so dirty and ashamed, she felt as if she needed her morning shower more than ever.

* * * *

Tina packed one bag. Sad that her whole life fit into one suitcase, but there it was. She knew Luann would take her in for a while. Her parents were easy that way. But she couldn't stay here, not for one more day, one more minute.

It had been the phone call. The thing that had finally moved her to action after years of hearing about her weight from her mother.

"I know, I can't wait for Vegas," her mother purred on the other line when Tina picked it up to call Luann. She hardly ever used the landline, but her cell phone had no

charge. She rolled her eyes at her mother's throaty laugh. What forty-something woman went off to Vegas with her girlfriends and left her husband home by himself, anyway? "I'm packing my sexiest lingerie just for you."

Tina stared at the phone, realizing her mother hadn't heard her pick up the extension—and her mother was definitely *not* talking to a girlfriend. Her suspicions were confirmed by the response that followed.

"Good." It was a masculine voice, deep and flirty. "I'm going to fuck you six ways to Sunday."

"Andrew!" Her mother laughed again, a girlish sort of giggle, and it made Tina wince. "I can't wait to get out of this house. David is driving me batshit and Tina doesn't do anything but mope around her room doing her homework."

"Doing homework sounds like a good pastime, if you ask me."

"Oh, I don't know." Her mother sighed. "I wish she'd get out more. Of course, I don't know who would ask her! She's so fat now, I'm afraid we're going to be stuck with her forever."

There was a pause. "Sounds like she didn't get her mother's lithe little body type."

"Decidedly not."

Tina hung the phone up quietly and carefully. She sat on her bed, motionless, for a long time. She didn't remember breathing or even blinking. The weight on her chest was far too heavy for that. When her stepfather poked his head in the door to say goodnight, she was still sitting there. And she didn't sleep at all, not that she remembered.

Her mother kissed her cheek and said goodbye in the morning—off to Vegas with the girls! *Yeah, right.* Tina swallowed the bile in her throat. Her own bag was already packed.

She saw the light on in his office and knew her stepfather must be in there. Her face flushed at the thought of him looking at porn while her mother flew off to Vegas with some guy. What was wrong with this picture? She felt

bad for him and stopped in the hallway, considering. Should she tell him? Did he know? Did it matter?

She lugged her suitcase down the stairs. It was the kind on wheels, which was good, because she would be walking a half-mile to Luann's house. She couldn't help remembering when she'd packed a bag at the age of seven, getting as far as the end of the block. Well this time, she really meant it.

"Running away?"

"Wh—what?" Tina gasped, her hand on the front doorknob, at the sound of her stepfather's voice coming from the darkness of the living room. She blinked when a lamp switched on, revealing him sitting there all alone on the couch. "I thought you were in your office…"

"Where you going?" His eyes met hers, and she remembered it had been her stepfather who had found her sitting on the porch with her satchel when she was seven, who had inquired—*whatcha runnin' from?* And of course she'd broken down and told him. She couldn't for the life of her remember the reason she'd given him.

Tina cleared her throat and lied. "Spending the night at Luann's."

"That's a big suitcase for an overnight trip." He raised an eyebrow, patting the sofa beside him. "Come here. Let's talk."

She knew instinctively it was a bad idea, but something drew her to his side. She slipped off her shoes and she left her bag and went to sit beside him. He smelled of aftershave—and alcohol. He slid an arm around her shoulder, pulling her head to his chest.

"Whatcha runnin' from, Teeny?"

Maybe it was because he used the same phrase he'd used when she was seven, sitting on the porch in her sundress with Sponge-Bob Band-Aids on each knee. Or maybe it was the nickname he resurrected, long dead and buried since puberty, when she started filling out and her

mother began with the incessant comments about her weight.

"I'm not teeny!" she protested, and immediately burst into tears. She felt him put his arms fully around her, and she let herself be held, comforted. His lips brushed her forehead, her temple, not talking, just riding it out, letting her feel what she was going to feel.

"I hate her," she whispered, her cheek to his chest, feeling the familiar rise and fall.

"Your mother?"

She nodded, wiping her cheeks. "She hates me. Nothing's good enough for her. I'm not smart enough, or pretty enough, or sk-sk-skinny enough..." She felt the tears coming again and fought them. "She's right. No man is ever going to want me."

"Don't say that." He squeezed his arms around her shoulders, shaking his head. "It's not true, Christina. You're beautiful."

"I am?" She lifted her head, eyeing him with suspicion. She couldn't help remembering the other night in his study. Had he really been thinking about her? It made her feel warm and...wanted. Really, *really* good.

"Of course you are."

"No I'm not." She rolled her eyes, that feeling gone in an instant. "I'm fat. Ugly."

"Trust me," he told her, his gaze moving down from her face to the peasant top she was wearing and the long, flowing skirt below it. "Some guy is going to very much appreciate those gorgeous curves of yours some day."

"I wish I was skinny," she lamented. "Like Mom."

"You know, you probably don't remember, but your mom didn't look like that when I met her." He reached into his back pocket—he was dressed casually for the weekend, jeans and a polo shirt—pulling out his wallet. They'd gotten married when she was a baby, so she didn't remember their wedding, and she'd never remembered seeing any wedding photos. "Look."

And now she knew why. "She's like me."

They could have been twins. Her mother had cleavage, and full, curvy hips. Even a bit of a belly! Of course, Tina had been a baby then, and she was probably still breastfeeding. No wonder...

"Mm-hmm." He smiled, slipping the photo back into his wallet. "She's gotten kind of obsessive about her weight over the years. But don't let her make that your problem. You're perfect, just the way you are."

She shook her head, but she was looking at him, trying to gauge his real feelings as she said, "I don't believe it."

"I know you don't." His fingers brushed her hair, the nape of her neck, making her shiver. "What can I do to convince you?"

She met his eyes, realizing how very close they were sitting. She was practically in his lap. She hadn't sat in his lap since she was a very little girl. And she wasn't a little girl anymore.

"Do you really want to know?" She shifted more toward him, her face turned up to his. She saw his eyes widen, the realization dawning in them, but she did it anyway, bridging the distance and pressing her lips to his. She didn't know what to expect—guilt, shame, certainly rejection—but she had a secret hope, one she hadn't admitted yet even to herself until that moment.

He kissed her back.

He kissed her back!

His hand moved behind her neck, his mouth opening hers with a soft groan, tongue exploring. He tasted like alcohol and she liked it, breathing in the scent of him, trying to get as close as possible, managing to wiggle her way sideways into his lap.

"Tina, no..." His voice was barely a whisper as she wrapped her arms around his neck, kissing him again and again, so hungry. "Please, don't..."

"Am I too heavy?" She felt a pain deep in her belly and she saw his shock at her words, knew he must have seen the hurt on her face.

"No!" He grabbed her around the waist, pulling her closer, and she felt his erection against her hip. "God no. You feel... so..." He took a deep, shuddering breath, looking up from her breasts, which were now at his eye-level, to her face, her hair falling softly around them, blocking out the light, cocooning them in heat. "So... fucking... good..."

His words thrilled her and she wiggled in his lap, hearing him groan, but feeling his cock respond, throbbing against the denim. "Please... show me."

"Show you?" He looked dazed, confused, as she took his hand, daring, not quite believing it herself, to bring it up to her breast.

"Show me... show me how beautiful you think I am," she urged, her mouth so close to his they were almost kissing. "Make me believe it."

"Oh god." He swallowed, shaking his head, but his hand moved on its own, cupping her flesh, thumbing her nipple through her blouse, making it stand at attention. "Sweetie, we shouldn't—"

Tina moaned softly, arching, giving him more of her ample breast, covering his protest with her mouth. It wasn't nearly enough, not even close, and she broke their kiss briefly so she could straddle him, pulling her blouse over her head and dropping it to the floor.

"Oh Jesus, Mary and Joseph." His gaze fell on her breasts, spilling over a bra that was far too small—her mother always bought her clothes a little too tight as incentive—so small that her areolas appeared above the cups, her nipples hard and straining to get loose.

"We can't do this." He looked up at her, shaking his head again, but his hands had a mind of their own. "Oh god, you're so fucking gorgeous." He licked his lips, his eyes glazing over as he fondled first one, then the other.

She knew his resolve was waning. She also knew boys liked her breasts—it was one feature she knew to play up—and she felt a surge of pleasure through her body when she pulled her bra down, letting her tits spill free into her father's hands. The look on his face was a mix of delirium and animal lust.

"Please," she whispered, watching his big hands try to contain the overspill of flesh. "Oh it feels so good..."

With a low sound, something between a growl and a groan, his mouth found her nipple, sucking it between his lips. She whimpered and began to grind her hips, unable to stop herself, as if the friction could rub away their clothes. His cock strained against the denim of his jeans, and her motion in his lap created an actual heat they could both feel.

"Oh Tina," he whispered, pressing her breasts together in his hands, flicking one nipple, then the other. "You're so fucking beautiful I can't stand it. I want you so much."

"You do?" She watched him rubbing his stubbly cheek against the tender flesh of her breasts.

He opened his eyes, frowning. "It's wrong, I know."

"No." She cupped his face in her hands. "I want you too." She didn't want him to say no—she couldn't bear his rejection, not now—so she grabbed his hand again, this time placing it between her legs. Her skirt gave him easy access and his eyes widened when he felt the hot, swollen heat of her pussy through the damp crotch of her panties.

"See?" She moved her hips, grinding her mound into his palm, watching the look on his face change from guilt to wonder to desire. "See how much?"

He didn't answer her, his fingers busy working their way under the elastic of her panties, searching through the soft, wiry hair of her pussy for her wet slit. She moaned when he found her clit with his thumb, easing it gently back and forth, his gaze never leaving her face.

"Feel good?" he inquired, a smile playing on his lips. She rocked her hips toward him, giving him more, wanting more, rising up fully on her knees in his lap.

"So very good," she murmured, her head going back as his thumb made flat, easy circles, his fingers probing, looking for her entrance. She moaned when he slid two fingers inside of her and she squeezed her muscles around him, moving her hips, beginning to fuck him back.

"Mmmm, good girl," he encouraged, his other hand moving up to her breast, pulling at her nipple, making her whole body sing. "You like that?"

"Yessss." She looked down at him with half-closed eyes, her breath coming so fast she couldn't catch it. "But I know what I'd like better."

He raised an eyebrow, asking the question without a word.

"Your cock inside of me." She leaned in and pressed her mouth to his ear. "I want you to fuck me, Daddy."

He groaned and grabbed her ass in both hands. Her pussy cried out at the absence of his fingers, but she didn't have much time to think because her stepfather was wrapping her legs around his waist, her arms around his neck, and carrying her up the stairs. She giggled against his neck, remembering he used to carry her up the stairs just like this when she was too sleepy to make the trip on her own. He hesitated at the top of the stairs, looking down the hall to her room, and then the other way, towards his own.

"Your bed," she urged, squeezing him between her thighs. "Fuck me in your bed."

His eyes lit up at the prospect and he carried her in there, nudging the door open with his knee and before she knew what was happening, they were rolling around in her parents' bed, kissing and tugging at each other's clothes with desperation.

"We so shouldn't be doing this," he panted, lifting his hips so she could tug his jeans down. "But I can't stop. You're so fucking beautiful."

His words were like fuel to the fire inside of her and she didn't resist at all when he pulled her skirt off, leaving her in

just panties on the bed. Now they were both stripped down to their underwear.

She was normally embarrassed by her body, ashamed for anyone to see it, but the look on his face when he saw her unclothed was intoxicating. He looked at her like he could devour her.

And then he did.

Tina gasped in surprise when his mouth covered her mound through her panties, his tongue lapping, making her squirm and writhe on the bed. No one had ever done that to her before and the sensation was incredible, but she was far too embarrassed to let him go on.

"No, Daddy, no," she protested, trying to push him away.

"Hold still." He growled, grabbing her hips and yanking her panties down her thighs. He breathed a soft sigh when he saw her pussy for the first time and then he was devouring her again, his tongue pushing between her swollen labia, finding the nub of her clit in an instant.

"Oh! Daddy!" she cried, her knees falling open as he licked her, his mouth fastened on her mound. "Oh no... no... ohhhhh. That's so good! Ohhhhh!"

"Mmmmm!" He encouraged her, licking faster, spreading her open with his fingers to stroke her slit up and down, searching for her entrance. She moaned when he slid two of them into her, just like he had on the couch, but his mouth was far, far better against her clit than anything she'd ever felt—including the electric toothbrush she had hidden in her underwear drawer.

"Oh Daddy... if you keep doing that, I'm... I'm...mmmmmmm..."

His fingers pressed deeper, making her quiver, and he paused for a moment to look up at her face. "Good girl. I want you to come for me. Come all over my face. Will you do that?"

She whimpered, flushing deeply. "I can't. Please, don't make me."

"Yes you can." He flicked his tongue over her clit, teasing. "Feel that?"

She nodded, biting her lip to keep from crying out, and then he sucked her clit between his lips, twisting his fingers inside her, and she couldn't help the way her hips thrust up to meet him.

"Ohhh baby girl, your pussy tastes so fucking good," he groaned, mashing his face against her flesh. His words made her flush with heat and pleasure. "I'm going to eat you until you come."

And he did just as he promised, not letting Tina roll away when she wanted to, not letting her escape the hot lash of his tongue, making her play with her breasts, telling her how much it turned him on to watch her, so she couldn't resist, sending hot sparks down to her aching pussy with every pinch of her nipples.

"Daddy!" she cried, the feeling rising with her hips, centered between her legs. "Oh god, Daddy, I'm going to come!"

He groaned against her pussy, shoving his fingers in and out of her and sucking her clit hard between his lips. Tina shuddered, her pussy clamping down on his pistoning fingers as she came and came, her contractions fast and hard at first, driving her hips up and up, until the sensation finally fluttered off into oblivion, leaving her gasping for breath in her father's arms.

"Such a good girl," he whispered against her ear as he moved on top of her. She knew what was coming and she was more than ready for it, opening her thighs for him, feeling the first press of his cock between them. Somewhere along the way, his underwear had disappeared. "Oh baby, you're the most beautiful girl in the world. I want you so much."

"Really?" She looked into his eyes, searching for the truth. "You aren't just saying that?"

"I've wanted you for so long," he confessed, groaning when she reached down to grab his cock. So hard! She

stroked his length gently, like she'd seen him do that night in his study.

"Me too, Daddy," she whispered into his ear, rubbing the head of his cock against her still-quivering clit. "I know you were thinking about me… in your office."

His head came up, eyes wide. "Wh—what?"

"I was under your desk the other night," she confessed, flushing, squirming beneath him. His cock twitched and swelled in her hand. "I sooo wanted to suck you, Daddy. It seemed like such a waste, because I wanted to swallow all your cum."

"Oh god." He lowered his head to her breasts, sucking and lapping at her nipples as she tugged at his cock. He lifted his head, his look almost pained, a question in his eyes.

"What?" she murmured, running a hand through his hair, still dark but graying at the temples. "What is it?"

He pressed her breasts together, biting his lip, and met her eyes. "I want to fuck your gorgeous tits. Please?"

"Oh yes!" She smiled, putting her hands over his, making the mounds on her chest rise. "They're very sensitive."

He came to her, eyes burning, cock pulsing, the head slick with her juices. She took him in her hand, rubbing her thumb over the tip, making him groan. She liked the way that made her feel. Powerful.

"Going to need a little more lubrication," she whispered, tugging him toward her mouth. He gasped when she took him between her lips, rolling her tongue all around the tip. She knew how to do this well enough, and she liked showing him, watching the pleasure twist his features. Grabbing his hips, she guided him deeper into her throat, coating him with saliva, sucking him so enthusiastically, his eyes rolled back into his head.

"Easy," he murmured, slowing her, easing out of her mouth. "I still want to fuck those beautiful tits."

"I want you to." Her eyes lit up with delight as he pressed her breasts together, slipping his cock into her cleavage. The sensation was nice—but the look of pleasure almost to the point of pain on his face was the most gratifying thing about it. He fondled her breasts, toying with her nipples, moving his hips and driving his cock into her flesh.

"Ohhhh yes," she whispered, licking her lips as he tweaked her nipples, fucking her tits, completely lost in the sensation. Her pussy ached and she pressed her thighs together, feeling her clit pulse in the swollen squeeze of her labia. "Oh god. Oh god. Don't stop."

He opened his eyes, looking down and seeing her face, a mask of pleasure, and focused his attention on the nipples in his fingers. "Sensitive, hm?"

"Yes, yes, yes," she moaned, hips rocking, the motion of his hips rocking her toward heaven. "Oh god, I'm gonna… I'm… ohhhhhhhh!"

"Oh sweet, sweet girl," he cried as her climax shook her whole body, curling her toes, closing her eyes and arching her back, his cock caught between the rise of her breasts, both of their hands together, pressing them tight together.

"Oh Daddy," she whispered, barely recovered, head spinning, the tip of his cock appearing at the top of her cleavage. She reached her tongue out, dizzy, trying to lick the head. "Ohhh, you're so hard. I wish you were inside of me."

He groaned, shaking his head, hips bucking toward her lips, pre-cum glistening at the tip. "Oh, no, baby, if I fuck you… god…" he panted, closing his eyes.

"Oh please," she begged, wiggling, reaching for his cock and squeezing it. "I want it so much."

"Oh fuck, I can't…"

She stroked him, still breathing from her orgasm, licking and sucking the head with such hunger it made both of them gasp.

"Pretty please?" she begged, never feeling more powerful in her life as she slipped his cock back and forth between her lips, his eyes burning into hers. "With sugar on top?"

"Fuck!" He relented with a loud moan, positioning himself over her, waiting, letting her guide him toward her throbbing flesh—but once he was inside of her, there was no more hesitation. He bucked his hips against hers, driving her into the bed, shaking the whole thing, the headboard hitting the wall over and over.

Tina wrapped her legs around him, her arms too, letting herself be carried away. She had never had an orgasm with a man's cock inside of her, but she loved being fucked, the sweet sensation of being filled. And she liked knowing her body was being used for his pleasure, that something about her was pleasing to him.

"Oh god, sweetheart," he panted in her ear. "Your pussy is so fucking hot... so tight... ohhhhh god... you're going to make Daddy come!"

"Come for me," she whispered, hot against his cheek, feeling the tickle between her legs rising to an impossible hum. "Oh... ohhhh... ohhhh Daddy! Oh god!"

"Mmmm yeah!" he growled, rolling his hips, grinding into her pussy. "Come on my cock! Come all over my cock, baby girl!"

And they came together, the both of them, sweaty and shuddering and crying out as one, the thick, pulsing eruptions from his cock spilling heat deep into her, warming her like nothing else could. She wrapped herself completely around him, gasping against his neck as her pussy spasmed around his length, each wet, electric throb asking for more, more, more.

When it was over, he cradled her in his arms, kissing her cheek and nose and mouth, telling her over and over again how beautiful she was. She flushed and squirmed under his praise, wanting so much to believe him, so afraid it would all disappear if she opened her eyes.

"I have to tell you something," she whispered, feeling his lips brush her temple.

He stilled, waiting. When she didn't speak, he asked, "Is it about your mother?"

Tina nodded, looking at him for the first time since they'd come together—her stepfather, the man she'd loved forever.

"If it's about Vegas, I already know." He pressed his lips together for a moment, tucking a stray strand of hair behind her ear. "You weren't the only one packing a bag tonight."

Her eyes widened, and then she smiled. "Want to run away together?"

"Did you really think I was going to leave without you, beautiful girl?"

"I'm not—" She began to protest but he kissed her quiet, convincing her with his touch, his breath, his body, that she was—his beautiful girl.

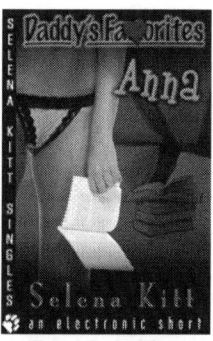

Anna (Daddy's Favorites)

For Anna, there was nothing like a comfortable, well-read, dog-eared book in her hands. She curled up at the end of the sofa, the TV on but forgotten, her feet tucked under an afghan, and lost herself in another world. She could do this for hours, and often did, only moving when her body reminded her of its needs. And even then, she would take her book to the bathroom, or if her stomach growled, she'd pour some cereal and continue reading, spoon in one hand, book in the other. Nothing could break the spell of a well-loved story playing out in her imagination.

"Anna!"

Well, almost nothing.

"What?" Anna yelled back at the ceiling, rolling her eyes and reaching for the remote so she could mute the television.

"Did you borrow my pearl earrings?" Her mother's voice floated down the stairs.

Anna turned her attention back to her book, not answering. She hadn't borrowed them, hadn't even seen them since the last time her mother wore them, some time in the fall. But of course, her mother wouldn't believe her, no matter what she said, so it was better not to say anything at all.

"Never mind!" her mother called down. "I found them!"

Anna sighed, hearing footsteps on the stairs. Her mother and stepfather were going to a Christmas party at her

stepfather's office. She couldn't wait for them to leave. She had half her book left to read, microwave popcorn waiting on the counter, and the number to Little Caesars memorized. She was set.

"Hey girlie." Her stepfather's voice interrupted her and she looked at him, pushing her glasses up her nose so she could see him better. Her BFF, Lizbeth, was always going on and on about how *freaking hawt* her stepfather was—and she wasn't wrong. Andrew Ross was a fine specimen of a man, tall and lean, dark hair and bright blue eyes. He always wore a suit to work, although on the weekends he put on jeans and cooked pancakes in his bare feet and the sight of him standing at the stove sometimes made her stomach do slow, sensuous flips.

"Hey." She returned his greeting, watching him pour a drink at the bar separating the living room and the kitchen. "Starting early?"

"Gotta keep myself occupied while your mother finishes up." He grimaced as he swallowed the amber-colored liquid.

Anna snorted, turning to her book again. "You could be drunk by then."

"Whatcha reading, girlie?" Drew inquired, coming over to the couch and sitting beside her, propping his feet up on the coffee table. Even though he'd technically been her stepfather for five years, she only called him "Dad" when her mother was around, and he was fine with that. He said he didn't mind her calling him by his first name, and so when they were alone, she often did.

"Pride and Prejudice." It was one of her all-time favorites. She shifted on the sofa, feeling his hand move under the blanket, squeezing her foot. It was a sweet, familiar gesture. There was nothing sexual about it really, but she felt her heart rate increase.

"Didn't you read that one already?" Drew tugged her bare foot out from under the covers, resting it in his lap, massaging gently.

"Several times." She was turned toward him now and she poked her other foot out from under the blanket so he could give it equal attention.

"Bookworm," he teased, switching to her other foot. Lifting it, he inspected her pink-painted toenails. "Cute. Like little bits of candy."

"Thanks." Anna settled back against the arm of the sofa, sighing softly as he massaged the sole of her foot. The other was resting in his lap. "It's called Aphrodite's Pink Nightie."

He raised his eyebrows and smirked. "I guess it has to be someone's job to make up nail polish flavors."

"It's colors not flavors." She shifted on the sofa, her book forgotten, watching him inspect her toes.

"I know," he agreed. He was enthralled, and she shivered at the way his hand moved up to her calf a little. "But they look good enough to eat."

"Omnomnom." She wiggled the foot still sitting in his lap, trying to make it seem casual, stretching and fake-yawning and she did so, and discovered something delightful—Drew had an erection. A very large erection.

He gasped, dropping her other foot. "Anna!"

"What?" She smirked. "I'm just getting comfortable."

"I think I hear your mother." Drew stood, going again to the bar to pour himself another drink. Anna curled back up with her book, but she left her toes uncovered.

"Ugh. Reading again?" Her mother appeared at the bottom of the stairs, hair pulled up, pearls at her throat. "It had better be a school book."

"At least she's reading." Drew poured himself another shot.

Anna's mother scoffed. "Did you see her grades? I don't know how she's going to graduate. And I'm not paying for summer school!"

"It's not a big deal."

"Obviously you don't think so."

Anna rolled her eyes, waiting for what was coming next, and she knew, of course, it was coming. Her mother wouldn't let an opportunity slip by. She turned to Anna, wagging a finger at her like she was still eight years old.

"What would it take for you to take it seriously? Should I call your father? Oh, wait, I can't—he's in Brazil with the whore!"

Anna stiffened, her eyes blazing. "Leave Daddy alone."

"Why should I?" her mother snapped. "That's where he left us—alone!"

"Okay, girls, let's dial it back a bit." Drew picked up his mother's coat—it was black mink, her mother didn't have any qualms about buying real anything—helping her into it. "Besides, I have an idea."

They both glowered at him. "What?"

"Well, when I was a kid, my parents used to pay me for my grades," he confessed, shrugging his own coat on.

Anna's mother snorted, rolling her eyes. "Oh please!"

"Hey, don't dismiss it. It actually works. Think about it—as adults, we have jobs, and the reason we do them is because there's a paycheck at the end of the week, right?"

"School isn't a job..." Anna's mother reminded him with a sniff, pulling on her gloves.

"Sure feels like it," Anna grumbled.

Drew smiled at her. "It kind of is, when you think about it. So why shouldn't she be rewarded if she does well?"

"Can she be penalized if she doesn't do well?"

Anna rolled her eyes. Of course her mother would think of something like that.

"I suppose..." Drew replied.

"Fine. If you don't make good grades, I take your car," her mother snapped.

Anna sat straight up, eyes wide. "What?"

Drew held out his hand in a halting gesture. "But if she does do well—say she'll get $100 for every A, $50 for every B and $25 for every C."

"But if you fail a class—just one class—" Anna's mother wagged her finger again.

"I won't." Anna was already doing the math. She had six classes, and if she could manage an A in all of them, that meant six-hundred dollars!

"So it's a deal?" Drew raised an eyebrow in her direction.

"It's a deal," she agreed.

"Shake on it." He took a step toward the couch, holding out his hand, and Anna took it, remembering his hands on her feet, the way he admired her painted toes. And his erection. Her gaze dropped to his trousers and then she looked back up at him, feeling a flush on her cheeks. Her face felt hot too and she wondered if she looked the same.

"I'll believe it when I see it." Anna's mother called from the doorway. "You be good!"

Drew joined his wife, remarking, "I'm sure she'll just read all night."

"Not too late. We have family pictures in the morning!" Those were the last words Anna's mother said before following her husband out the door.

Ugh. We don't have a family.

Anna grabbed her book, opening it to the dog-eared page she'd left off at, but she couldn't concentrate. She was thinking about the new deal she'd just made with her stepfather. School had never been that important to her, she had to admit. But six-hundred dollars! Now that was what she called an incentive, especially since her mother loved to spend money on herself, but was tight with it the rest of the time. It was almost a new year, she reminded herself. She could make a resolution and stick to it. She was sure she could.

* * * *

"You're up late." Anna was on her way to the kitchen for a late night snack when she found her stepfather stretched out on the couch, the TV on but muted.

Drew glanced back at her. "Can't sleep."

"She's asleep?" Anna wandered over to the sofa, looking down at him wearing just a pair of jeans, bare feet propped up on the arm of the couch.

He snorted. "Passed out is more like it."

She saw the way his gaze moved over her. The pink baby doll nightie she was wearing didn't conceal very much. She'd overheard him arguing with her mother just a few weeks ago about what she "flounced around the house" wearing. He said it bothered him, that she should be more modest. But she knew the truth—he liked it. She caught him watching her all the time.

Her mother had scoffed at his protest, but her mother was blind. She seemed to think that Drew was still her young, handsome personal assistant—which is how they'd met in the first place—not her husband. She ordered him around, picked his clothes, told him who to see, who not to see. Her mother didn't acknowledge Drew now owned his own business, that he was no longer her subservient, but her equal. It made Anna sick.

"Drew, I've been thinking about your proposition." Anna played with the hem of her nightie, seeing his gaze move there, over the creamy, pale skin of her thighs. He'd been drinking. She could smell it. But of course, he'd started before they even left for the party.

"What proposition?" He cleared his throat, sitting up on the sofa.

"You know, cash for grades?"

"Oh, that." He looked relieved and rubbed his eyes, yawning. "Yeah, what about it?"

"What if I don't want cash? What if I want something else instead?"

He frowned. "Like what?"

"I've seen you looking at me."

His eyes widened. "Anna..."

"You want to see more don't you... Daddy?"

She never called him Daddy unless her mother was around. The word in her mouth made what she was about to

do seem even more taboo. Anna grabbed the edge of her nightie and pulled it slowly over her head. Drew sat, transfixed, as she cupped her breasts, pushing them up and together in her bra. The hungry look in his eyes made her even bolder and she edged closer to him on the couch, her skirt riding up her thighs, until she was practically sitting in his lap.

"Do you like what you see so far?" Anna thumbed her nipples, shivering. They were hard, tenting the pink fabric of her bra. He didn't answer her, but he didn't have to. She saw Drew looking at her hands moving over her breasts, slowly pulling down her bra, letting it play peek-a-boo with her nipples. "Do you want to touch me?"

Anna turned on the sofa, sliding her leg over both of his, straddling him. Drew groaned softly, not touching her, but not stopping her either. He looked up past the swell of her breasts, her nipples appearing just above the lace edge of her bra, meeting her eyes, and his expression was beyond words. There was something wild and desperate in that look she wanted to reach.

She leaned in close so her lips brushed his ear. "I think about you when I touch myself."

His breath caught and his hands went to her hips. She thought he would push her off, reprimand her, but instead he pulled her gently against his pelvis so she could feel the length of his cock through his jeans. He was very hard and Anna's pussy lips parted around the outline of his shaft, even through her panties, as if she could suck him into her.

"Do you think about me, Daddy?" She wiggled in his lap, shifting back and forth, side to side, rubbing the aching bud of her clit against the seam of his jeans. "When you're with my mother, are you wishing it was my little pussy you were fucking?"

She knew it was true; it had to be. But she wanted—needed—to hear him say it. Drew's hands moved over her hips, around to her ass, cupping her behind through her sheer, matching pink panties and pulling her in tight. He

groaned, finding himself face to face with the swell of her breasts, spilling completely over her pink bra cups now.

"Fuck, Anna," he groaned as she arched, offering her tits to him like a gift. "What are you doing?"

"I think you know," she whispered, lifting one of her breasts and pointing a nipple toward his mouth. "You want me. I know you do. I can read you like a book."

"Oh hell." He swallowed, pursing his lips as if he could keep her at bay, her nipple brushing over his mouth, his chin.

"Tell me, Daddy." She cupped both breasts, pressing them together, rubbing her nipples over his rough, reddened cheeks. "Tell me you want me. You want me more than her."

"Fuck! Yes!" He swore again, thrusting his hips toward the ceiling, taking her with him, hands still firmly pressing her into his crotch. "Yes! Yes! I want to fuck you. Is that what you want to hear?"

"Yes." She smiled, satisfied, as he lowered his hips, bringing her back down, his breath hot against her breasts. He caught a nipple in his mouth, sucking deeply, and she gasped, twisting in his arms, pulling out of his grasp.

"What are you doing?" His breath was coming fast, just as fast as hers, as she slid down to kneel between his thighs. She unzipped him before he could protest, freeing his cock. He was hard, the tip of his cock wet with precum. She rubbed it in with her thumb before taking him into her mouth. Drew moaned, watching her with an expression caught between bliss and disbelief.

"Where did you learn to do that?" he murmured, pushing her hair out of the way so he could watch.

Anna let him slip briefly from between her lips to answer. "You can learn a lot from reading books."

"Show me."

She did, swallowing his length again and again, rubbing the head of his cock over her lips and flicking at it with her tongue when she felt his thighs start to tremble and his hips

rise. She made it last, wanting to explore him with her mouth, every glorious inch. His cock was thick, a nice, respectable length, the circumcised head fat and spongy against her tongue.

"Easy, girlie." His hand in her hair slowed her when she got too excited. "Not yet."

"I'm so wet," she murmured, licking down his shaft, flicking her tongue at the base of his cock.

"Touch yourself," he urged, looking down at her hard nipples brushing against his inner thigh.

Her pussy was wet, the crotch of her panties soaked, and she pushed them aside so she could rub her clit, moaning softly as she gently sucked the head of his cock. Drew watched her face, eyes half-closed, lost in his own pleasure but still paying attention to hers.

"I want to see you," he insisted, tugging at her hair. "Stand up. Show me."

Anna flushed, but she did as he asked, using his knees to steady herself. She showed him her pink panties, how they were pushed aside into the crook of her thigh, her pussy lips shaved smooth. His eyes lit up at the sight and his fisted his cock as she parted her lips with one hand and made circles around her clit with the other.

"You're so beautiful," he whispered, licking his lips. "Would you let me taste you?"

"Maybe." She smiled, her knees weak at the thought.

"Come here." He reached for her, helping her step up onto the sofa, one foot on each side of him.

Reaching around, Drew found the zipper to her skirt and slid it down. She stepped carefully out of it, assuming the same position. He grabbed her hips, guiding her toward his mouth, and Anna gave in to him, her knees buckling slightly. He took the weight of her on his shoulders, his hands moving over her body as he fastened his mouth over the wet flesh of her pussy.

"Oh god," she whispered, her eyes closing involuntarily. She'd had boys do it to her before like this, but she'd never

had anyone so skilled. Drew's tongue was relentless, flicking back and forth against her clit, teasing at first, testing her reaction. When she moaned and thrust her hips at him, rocking toward his tongue, he slid his arms under her legs and ass, palms pressed to the small of her back, and began to suck her clit.

"Ohhhhh Drew," she whispered, tweaking her own nipples to heighten the sensation, knowing it wouldn't be long, not long at all, before she was flooding his tongue with her juices.

He stopped just long enough to gasp, "Call me Daddy."

"Daddy," she whispered, a smile playing on her lips, a thrill going through her. "Oh Daddy, that's so good. Lick my pussy, Daddy. Make your baby girl come all over your face."

"Ohhhh fuck!" Drew's words were muffled but she understood them clearly enough. Then there were no more words at all, because he was drowning in her flesh, devouring her pussy with mouth and tongue and teeth, driving her toward orgasm.

"Daddy!" she cried, knowing now it thrilled him as much as it did her. "Oh Daddy! Daddy! You're going to make me come!"

"Mmmm!" was his only response, aside from the flickering pass of his tongue over her sensitive clit. She was so close, thighs trembling, her body completely his, and then she was coming, shuddering and spreading wide as his mouth took her places she thought she'd been but had never really seen, not like this. The world was all bright light and sound and pure, pulsing pleasure.

"Ohhhhh Daddy," she whispered as she began to come back down to earth, collapsing onto the sofa, straddling him again, this time in a sitting position.

"Kiss me." He didn't wait for her to answer. He cupped her face in his hands and kissed her, forcing his tongue onto her mouth, making her taste herself. Anna protested at first,

but his mouth was so sure, his tongue softly exploring, and she gave in, sharing the musky taste of her pussy with him.

"I want you," she whispered, rubbing herself against him. His cock was caught between them, hard and pulsing. Her labia parted for his length and she rubbed her clit up and down the shaft, shivering at the sensation. "I want you to fuck me, Daddy. Please."

He groaned, shaking his head. "We can't."

"Please." Anna felt him giving in and pressed on. "Please, oh god, please, I want it."

"You haven't gotten your report card yet," he teased, biting his lip as she rolled her hips.

"Do you mean it?" She rocked, back and forth, the wetness of her pussy making a slick path for his cock, up and down her slit. "If I get all As, will you fuck me?"

He groaned. "You could make me come like that."

"Do you want me to?" She brightened, moving faster. They were both panting.

"I want to come on your hot little pussy."

"Right here?" Her fingers found her clit, rubbing it as she rocked and rolled, watching the pleasure on his face. "Like this? Is this good?"

"Perfect."

"Faster?"

He nodded, holding onto her hips. "A little faster."

"Harder?"

"Oh god." He gasped when she grabbed his shaft in her fist, pumping him against her clit, rubbing the head over her sensitive nub. "Yeah, baby girl, that's good. Tug on Daddy's cock."

"Ohhhh." Her pussy quivered, so close, so very close. "You feel so good Daddy. I want your cum all over my wet cunt."

"Oh fuck!" He gave into it, moaning loudly, thrusting into her hand, right against her wet pussy. "Anna! Oh!"

"Yes, Daddy! Yes!" His cum was hot, shooting in thick spurts against her clit, and the sensation sent her over the

edge. She shuddered against him, whimpering as her orgasm shook her whole body, and Drew held onto her tight, letting her collapse in his arms.

"Now what?" In the aftermath of what she'd done, Anna flushed, hiding her face in his neck. But oh, he was so warm, he felt so good, his strong arms wrapped around her.

"Now you get to bed, young lady, before your mother wakes up and finds out what we've been up to." He squeezed her behind and slid her onto the sofa. Both of them began to straighten their clothing, repairing the damage.

Anna got up, ready to head upstairs, but she couldn't help herself, turning around and leaning down to kiss him softly on the mouth. "I won't tell. I promise."

"You're a bad girl," he replied hoarsely.

"The baddest." She smirked. "Do I need a spanking?"

He hand came down hard against her bottom and she squealed, eyes widening.

"To bed," he insisted.

"Yes, Daddy." She felt his gaze on her the whole way.

* * * *

Anna cradled her cell phone, whispering to Lizbeth. "They're still fighting."

"Still?" Her friend was chewing something loudly. "At this rate, they're gonna divorce by the time you graduate next month and you won't get any money at all!"

Anna had told her about her report card deal and the possibility of cashing in. She was on track to get all As. Of course, she hadn't told her about the other, secret deal she'd made with her stepfather.

"So what are they saying?" Lizbeth crunched into the phone.

Creeping to the door, Anna opened it a crack, hearing their voices rising up the stairs. "Caroline, I'm not an idiot. You really expect me to believe this guy on Facebook you decided to meet for drinks without telling me is 'just a old friend?'"

"I don't care what you believe!" Anna's mother snapped. "It's the truth. If you can't trust me, that's your problem!"

There was more, but Anna shut the door again, relaying the new information to Lizbeth.

"Damn. Your mom's cheating? Why in the hell would she cheat on Drew? He's so fucking *hawt*!"

Anna didn't tell her just how much she happened to agree with her. "Hey, someone's coming upstairs, I gotta run."

She heard their door open and close at the end of the hall. Downstairs, a car pulled out of the driveway. Anna peeked out the window and discovered her mother's car gone. Opening her bedroom door, she listened, but didn't hear anything.

"Hello?" she called hesitantly, taking cautious steps toward their room and then knocking quietly. "Is anyone home?"

The door opened and there was Drew, his mouth set in a grim line. She looked past him and saw a suitcase sitting open on the bed. It was stuffed haphazardly with his clothes. Her head was filled with a similar vision of her father, ten years earlier, packing a different suitcase.

"What are you doing?" she whispered, wide-eyed.

"Leaving." He turned around, stalking back into the room, and began pulling his clothes out of dresser drawers.

Anna sat on the edge of the bed, watching him shove his stuff into the suitcase. He couldn't leave. He just couldn't. What was she going to do without him?

"Don't go." She heard the tremble in her voice, but she couldn't help it. "Please. Don't leave me."

Drew stopped in the middle of zipping his suitcase, his expression softening as he looked at her. "Oh sweetheart... I'm not leaving you. I'm leaving your mother."

"But you're leaving." Anna felt tears welling.

"I'm sorry." Drew sat on the bed beside her, putting an arm around her shoulders. "It's just... it's not working out between me and your mom."

Anna turned to face him, putting her arms around his neck, and he hugged her, kissing the top of her head. When she lifted her face to his, their mouths were very close. She could smell alcohol on his breath.

"Take me with you," she breathed. "Please."

"Oh Anna..." He sighed, shaking his head. She knew what his answer was going to be, but she knew too she could change his mind. She was sure of it.

She closed the gap between them, touching her lips to his. He stiffened, starting to pull away, but she clung too tightly, climbing into his lap like she had that night on the sofa. They hadn't talked about it since, but it was always there, a secret between them, every time he saw her changing in her room (she left the door open when they were the only ones home) and then there was the time she caught him jerking off in the bathroom. He'd called her name when he came, opening his eyes to see her standing there in the doorway with her hand stuck down her panties. *It should have happened then*, she thought. It should have happened that first night on the couch. But somehow he had resisted. They both had.

But not now. Not anymore.

"Anna, no!" Drew panted as she fumbled with his zipper, reaching in to unleash his cock. It was as hard as she'd imagined, and she was on it before he could say another word, sucking and licking, hungry for him. His hand moved in her hair, trying to push her away at first, but it was no use. Her mouth was fastened over him, taking as much of him as she could.

"I want it so much," she whispered, unzipping her own jeans one-handed and shoving her hand into them. Her pussy was sopping wet. "Oh god, please, Drew. Please."

She looked up at him, begging with her eyes, her mouth, her hand stroking his cock, and still saw the hesitation on his

face. Anna stood, determined, sliding her jeans down over her hips and stepping out of them, peeling her t-shirt off. She was in just a bra and panties now and the greedy look in her stepfather's eyes was more than encouraging.

"Touch me." She lifted his hand, pressing it to her breast over her bra. Drew groaned, rubbing his thumb over her hard nipple through the material. She shivered, moaning softly, her hand slipping under the elastic of her panties so she could play with herself. "Oh god yes... that's so good. You make my pussy so wet."

He moaned again at her words, closing his eyes, shaking his head, but his body was betraying him, his hands traveling down her ribcage, her hips, pulling her into his lap. She straddled him happily, rocking against his cock, just like she had that night on the sofa, and Drew kissed her, drawing her tongue into his mouth, sucking gently as he kicked off his jeans and boxers.

"Oh Anna, sweetheart," he whispered, looking down to see her pussy exposed, panties aside, the entrance just inches from the head of his dick. "I can't. We can't. Ohhh fuck."

"Yes," she insisted, pushing him back on the bed. The suitcase was beside them, packed and ready to go. "Yes, we can. Fuck me, Drew."

He looked up at her sitting on top of him, her hand moving the head of his cock through her slit, coming dangerously close to her hole. Her pussy spasmed, as if it could draw him into her.

"You know you want it." She slapped the head of his dick against her pussy. "You want to fuck my wet little cunt."

"Anna!" he cried, shaking his head, but she knew her words were getting to him.

"Yes, Daddy," she murmured, hearing him make a sound that was almost a sob. "You want to fuck your little girl's wet pussy, don't you?"

"Ohhhh fuck." His hands tightened on her hips, face twisted into a grimace. "Ohhhh yes. Yes! I want your cunt! Put it in, Anna! Put it in!"

Triumphant, she did, sliding down onto his cock in one long, fluid motion. They both cried out at the sensation, and Anna leaned over to kiss him, slanting her mouth across his in a desperate kiss.

"I'm going to fuck you, little girl," he murmured, his hips already rolling under hers. "I'm going to fuck you so fucking good."

She moaned as he bucked her up, rolling her onto the bed and driving into her. Anna gasped, wrapping her arms around his neck, her legs around his waist, as he fucked her hard and deep, giving her all the pent up lust they'd been holding back for months—for years.

"Ohhh yes, Daddy!" She fucked him back, as hard as she could. "Do it hard! I love it hard like that! Oh yesss!"

He grunted and thrust, grinding his pelvis into hers. "Oh Anna, your fucking pussy is so good. I'm gonna come! I'm gonna come, sweetheart. Ahhhh god!"

"Yes!" She arched her back, hands fisted in his hair, feeling her own orgasm just seconds behind. "Oh Daddy, make me come all over your big fucking cock!"

That did it for both of them, and Drew shuddered and slammed into her one last time, sending her over the edge of darkness into light, the world exploding around them both. She felt every pulse as he filled her, every sweet wave of his cum, and her spasming pussy welcomed it all.

"Oh Anna." He kissed her cheek, her mouth, her chin, her neck. "Oh fuck. I'm so sorry. I'm so, so sorry."

"Don't apologize," she murmured, stroking his hair, still dizzy, her ears ringing. "Just take me with you."

He lifted his head, looking down at her with soft eyes. "Oh god, girlie. If we did that... I don't even want to think what might happen."

"Anything." She smiled, kissing his cheek. "We could be... oh Drew, we could be everything to each other. We could run off and be together and... and find some happy."

Drew chuckled. "Find some happy?"

"That's what Lizbeth says. She says if you're not getting it where you're at, you should go find yourself some happy." Anna wanted this, wanted him, more than she ever could have said. Now that she was faced with losing him, she knew it more than she ever had before. She just didn't know if he felt the same way about her.

He has to. He just has to.

He looked at her for a long time, not saying anything and she felt herself trembling, hoping beyond hope.

"I love you, Anna."

She blinked back tears. "I love you too, Drew."

"What was I thinking?" He lowered his head to her neck and she felt him give a little sob and her heart lurched in her chest, hope fading. And then he said something she could have only dreamed of hearing. "I couldn't leave you, girlie. I could never leave you."

"So you'll take me with you?" she asked, breathless.

He groaned, sounding like a man in pain. "Yes. Fuck it. Yes, yes, yes. Pack your bags, sweetheart. Let's go find ourselves some happy."

Christa (Daddy's Favorites)

His wife had her period panties and her regular ones—and then there were those tucked in the way back of the drawer. Those were the ones Jim was hunting for.

He found a pair he thought she might consider wearing—white satin with a red lace trim, the tag still dangling from the edge. He ripped off the plastic tab, tucking the tag into his pants pocket, wondering if these were the pair he had bought for her last Valentine's Day. They looked like something he would buy her, sexy but tasteful. Rachel hated anything slutty.

He put them on the bed, along with the dress and the card, jumping when he heard the door slam downstairs. "Dad?"

"I'll be down in a minute!" he called. It was just his stepdaughter home from the Ashley's—he heard her defiant tread on the stairs, coming to find him anyway. *Note to self: tell the eighteen-year-old the opposite of whatever you want them to do.* Jim edged out of the bedroom, shutting the door and meeting Christa at the top of the stairs. She was carrying her backpack over one shoulder, and she blew a wisp of long blond hair out of her eye as she smiled up at him.

"Hey, Dad." Christa gave him a one-armed hug as she slipped by him. "Can I sleep over at Ashley's tonight?"

Jim startled. He was going to ask her that very question! "Sure," he replied, surprised at how well that had worked out, although he shouldn't have been. It was the weekend,

after all, and she seemed to spend every waking moment attached at the hip with her best friend. "Your mother and I are going out tonight."

"Ewwwwww, then I'm definitely going to Ashley's." Christa wrinkled her freckled nose, and Jim smiled. She looked exactly like her mother when she did that.

"What's that supposed to mean?" Jim asked, heading down the stairs.

"You know!" Christa called back, making squeaking sounds. "Ee-eee-eee-eee-eee!"

Jim flushed, looking back over his shoulder, recognizing her attempt at the imitation of the sounds of the mattress he shared with her mother, but Christa was already in her room. "You can hear us?" he asked, thinking it had been so long, he couldn't really remember the last time he and Rachel had made love.

"Well, only the bed, actually," she replied, peeking her head around the corner. "Which is good, really, because Ashley's mom sounds like Lassie, you should hear her! Owwww-owwwww-owwwwwwwwoooo!" Christa howled and then giggled.

"Christa!" Jim tried to make sure he intoned the right amount of disapproval.

"Oh, Dad, you should hear the words she uses!" Christa said, her eyes widening. "I can't even repeat them to you!"

"You shouldn't," he agreed, turning fully toward her on the stairs now, his hand gripping the rail. "What does she say?"

"Dad!" Christa's complexion pinked, but her blue eyes were dancing, as if delighted with his question.

"Okay." He shrugged, moving to go. "Just curious. You can tell me if you want."

"Wait!" Christa lowered her voice to a conspiratorial tone. She came and plopped herself down on the top stair, tucking her hair behind her ears and looking past him as if she were afraid someone might hear her. "Dad, she says the naughtiest things, you wouldn't believe me if I told you!"

"Try me," Jim replied, shifting his weight on the stairs. He was wearing dress slacks that didn't hide an erection very well, and he could feel himself beginning to stiffen at the thought of dirty talk. Standing here looking at Christa's milk-white thighs splayed open to show the crease of her sex in red jogging shorts wasn't helping the situation much either, he mused.

Christa was really blushing now, and her voice rose an octave as she repeated, "Oh David, fuck me harder! Oooo yeah, I can take it all! That's it, baby, slam your prick into my hot cunt!"

Jim's eyes widened as he listened to her, breath caught in his throat, his cock straining against his underwear. "Okay, Christa." He turned his back to her, not willing to risk her seeing how hard she had just made him. "Enough."

"You said you wanted to hear." She pouted, flouncing up the stairs and going back to her room.

"Thanks for sharing," he called back over his shoulder as he turned the corner toward the kitchen. Jim leaned against the counter, cheeks flushed, cock throbbing. Jesus, all those nasty words out of Christa's mouth! He closed his eyes for a moment, trying to imagine Rachel saying anything like it, and simply couldn't.

Maybe tonight, he thought, shifting the bulge in his pants and getting the bottle of wine from the counter. He set up two glasses and sat down at the table, willing his heart to stop beating so fast. From here, he could see the Parker house, which was parallel to the Stevens' on the next block, where Ashley and her apparently raunchy mother lived. Jim had seen her on many occasions over the years, but he never would have guessed that Linda Stevens could open up her mouth and say anything close to the string of words Christa had put together upstairs. He wondered if she had just been putting him on.

He saw the headlights of Rachel's Intrepid appear on the garage door, and he smiled, imagining her gathering up her purse, her bag with all her lesson plans. It was such a sweet

moment of anticipation, the time between knowing she was home and waiting for her to appear. The side door opened and she swept in carrying a hamster cage, complete with hamster.

Jim stood, his eyebrows raised as he moved instinctively to help her. "Uh, what's this?"

She let him take the cage and he looked around for the best place to put it, deciding on the counter. Jim peered in at a little sleeping ball nearly the color of peach fuzz curled into one corner.

"Taffy, remember?" She began unslinging purses and bags from her shoulder, hanging them over a kitchen chair. "Classroom hamster. Jody Cornwell was supposed to take him home over spring break, but he has the chicken pox, and I couldn't get anyone else's parents' permission in time. Poor little guy had to wait in the car while I was visiting with Kathy after work—uh, and what's this?"

Rachel stood staring at the glasses and the wine and looked up at him, pushing her dishwater blond hair out of her face and frowning. Jim had used the corkscrew when he got home, careful to avoid an unmasculine display, just in case. He uncorked the bottle and began to pour them each a glass.

"We're celebrating." He offered her a glass of wine.

She smiled, her eyes questioning, and shook her head. "You know I don't like this stuff."

"Try it," he said, clinking his glass with hers.

"What are we celebrating?" She lifted the glass to her nose, wrinkling it at the smell. Jim smiled, seeing again the resemblance between Rachel and his stepdaughter.

He waited, watching her sip it, her eyes surprised as she took her first taste. "It's good, isn't it? We are going out to dinner, just the two of us."

"But what's the occasion?" She took another sip. "This isn't bad. Fruitier than most of the wine you've made me drink." She winked at him. "But it still tastes like alcohol."

Rachel sat at the kitchen table, kicking off her heels. As often as she complained about them, she still wore them, and Jim liked imagining her standing in front of a classroom of kindergarteners in those heels. She looked up at him, waiting.

Jim took a gulp of his wine. "We're going to see my play."

"Your... play?" Rachel set her glass on the table and stared at him.

Jim began talking fast. "It's a long story, really, but I wrote it just after our honeymoon, and it was sitting up there gathering dust, and I took it out in January, when I made that New Year's resolution to start writing again, remember?"

Rachel nodded, and inclined her head at him to continue.

Jim took another gulp of wine. "Well, it's kind of funny how it all fell into place. I mentioned I was writing more than just copy to John, and he told me he was doing his photography again, and he'd entered his photos into some contest."

Rachel stood, taking her glass to the sink.

Jim continued. "And he won something, actually. Anyway, I mentioned the play, and he told me about a woman he met who was starting a sort of dinner theater and she was looking for original plays."

Rachel poured the rest of her wine down the sink, rinsing the glass and setting it on the counter next to the hamster cage. "So what's this have to do with you?"

"Well, she liked my play and she said she wanted to direct it," he replied, pouring himself another glass of wine.

Rachel turned to him, crossing her arms over her chest. "And you want to do this?"

"Well, I kind of already did." He avoided her eyes and took another gulp from his glass.

"Jim," she sighed. "Is this, you know... one of *those* kinds of plays?"

"Well, yeah." He stood and put his arms around her waist. "It's an erotic kind of thing."

Rachel rested her head on his chest with a sigh, holding completely still. "Well, I guess that tells me what you think of my opinion."

"Come on, Rach. I was hoping you'd be excited, even a little proud..." Jim hugged her, kissing the creamy part in the middle of her platinum hair.

"Of what? You writing dirty stories?" She sniffed, shaking her head.

"I—" Jim was about to deny it and stopped. "I know how it makes you feel. I didn't want to make you—" He shrugged, searching for the word. "Uncomfortable?"

She raised her eyes to meet his and Jim felt an urge kiss her perfect little mouth in a way he never had before—he wanted to smear her pale pink lip gloss over her face and grind his lips into hers until she gasped. But he knew better.

Still, she was so naturally beautiful, her eyes like blue glass as they searched his face for something, her cheeks already slightly pink at the mention of what she termed "naughty stuff." It was an endearing term, and she was dear to him, but their short courtship and just ten-month marriage had him wondering if his appetite had already changed. Maybe that was what all the erotica writing was about, his craving for another flavor, a different color, something spicy with his sweet.

"I really don't want to have any part of it, Jim." She looked up, blinking at him. "Don't you understand that?"

"Come on, Rach..." He hugged her shoulders but she shrugged him off.

"No." She took a step back, frowning. "It's not okay with me. I don't like that you did it, I don't like that you hid it from me. I just don't like it. You know, Brian never would've done anything like this. Never."

He didn't say anything about her reference to her perfect ex-husband. Sometimes he wondered why she'd ever divorced him in the first place. But of course he knew—

Brian Davis had left her for another woman, a dancer. Someone exotic. More exciting, he imagined. But he wasn't going to tell her that.

"Please. Listen, we've got to go in about half hour," he admitted, looking at his watch. "We need to be there by six."

"You need to be there. *I'm* not going anywhere." She didn't even look at him as she passed, and he heard her climbing the stairs, pausing to talk to Christa. He thought of her reading the card and poured himself another glass of wine. He lifted his glass to the hamster cage.

"Here's lookin' at you, Taffy," he said, drinking it and wishing it was a shot of whiskey. He tapped on the glass, and the hamster yawned, showing its long teeth before turning and snuggling back into the little nest it had made for itself in the cedar.

When he went upstairs to ask her once more to come with him, he found her in the bathroom with the door locked and the tub running. On their bed, the card had been ripped into tiny pieces and the lingerie he'd left out had been shredded with a pair of scissors. The dress remained untouched.

Jim left it all, straightening his tie in the full-length mirror on the back of their bedroom door before heading out. He stopped at the bathroom, knocking gently. He noticed Christa's light still on and wondered why she hadn't left for Ashley's yet. Probably still chatting on her cell phone.

"Rach? I'm leaving. Aren't you at least going to tell me to break a leg?"

No answer. He sighed, turning to go, and then heard her call, "I hope you actually do!"

* * * *

The play was such a success, he stayed far too long drinking at the after-party backstage, so long he was afraid he might get arrested for drunk driving on the way home. *Although that might be preferable to facing Rachel,* he

mused, opening the driver's side door of his Audi and sliding in. The car still retained the heat of the day—spring in Texas, he'd discovered in the past ten months, was *hot*, especially for a man used to the northern temperatures of New England.

He'd grown up in Massachusetts, which was where he'd met his future wife at a local coffee house, while he was spending the summer teaching college courses and she was visiting relatives. It turned out she'd been licking her wounds after her marriage breakup, and the courtship had been a whirlwind affair. He'd fallen for her hard, so hard he'd given up his teaching position, found work doing editing from home, and had married her and moved to Texas, all without ever even meeting her teenage daughter or seeing their new home.

Christa had been shocked when she arrived home from a summer at her father's in California to find a new man living in her house. He couldn't blame the kid. He could hardly believe it himself. Both his mother and his sister had railed against his decision, but he wouldn't hear any of it. Rachel was the one. He'd been looking for someone like her his whole life, had remained unmarried, if not unattached, waiting for the right woman to walk into his life, and she finally had. The first time he saw her, that china doll face, her blonde hair, like an angel, the sweetest vision of his life, he just knew.

And then he'd met his new stepdaughter.

Jim quickly inserted the key so he could turn on the air conditioning. Images from the play he'd written soon after meeting his new stepdaughter ran through his head on a loop, all bright and sultry and hot. He'd written a good play, and the audience had shown their appreciation with two curtain calls, where a Lolita-type affair ended rather happily, instead of in tragedy, although the girl in question was, of course, of legal age. *Lolita couldn't be published in today's politically correct climate,* he thought, flipping the vent up

so it blew directly on his flushed face. He was drunk. Far too drunk to drive.

The thought of climbing into the backseat and sleeping it off occurred to him just at the same moment that Christa's tousled blond head popped up between the seats behind him, like something from a horror movie. He yelped—giving himself credit for not screaming outright like a girl—and twisted around to look at her.

"What in the hell are you doing here?"

She rubbed her sleepy eyes and yawned. "I came to see your play."

"How did you—?" But of course he knew. His argument with Rachel hadn't been quiet. Christa had overheard them. "...get here?" He finished his sentence differently than it had started out, watching, bemused, as Christa began to climb through the seats to the front. She tossed a pair of heels over first and then slid a slender, pale thigh through the narrow opening between the seats, wiggling her way through, climbing over the console.

"Ashley came with me." Christa rolled her eyes at his shocked expression, settling herself into the passenger seat. "Don't worry I didn't tell her it was *your* play. I told her I was meeting a boy." Christa turned toward him in the dimness, the circle of a streetlight making her eyes gleam. "She thought it was *totally* perverted, by the way."

Jim felt heat creeping into his cheeks. "And what did you think?"

"I thought it was fucking hot." She grinned, propping her bare foot up on the seat, fully facing him now, unladylike in her dress, letting her slim thighs part, giving him a view of her panties. The dress was an elegant little black number, but her panties were plain white cotton. Her mother bought them for her, he knew. They were exactly Rachel's taste.

"Christa!" He was very glad for the darkness, both because of the redness of his face and because of, god help him, the erection beginning to tent his trousers.

"What?" She laughed as he reached for the gearshift, making the car lurch as he pulled out of the parking lot. "Isn't that what you wanted? For people to get off? That girl went around in her underwear for half the play! Why did you name her Crystal?"

"I liked the name." Jim shifted his Audi into a higher gear as he merged onto the highway. He liked driving a stick-shift, liked the control it gave him. He was careful to observe all posted speed limits.

"Uh-huh." Christa laughed again, soft and knowing. She fished her purse from the back, and Jim couldn't help glancing over as she did, her skirt riding high up her thighs, revealing the tender, rounded curve of her ass under those cotton panties, the stretch of her tendons behind the knee, bare pink-painted toes curled against the dashboard as she reached and panted, searching the backseat.

"Found it!" she announced, plopping back into her seat, both feet up on the dash now. "Sorry I didn't tell you I was coming, but I felt bad when Mom said she wouldn't. I thought one of us should show up and support you."

"Well..." How could he fault her? In fact, he was proud and pleased she'd shown up. He glanced over as she fished a pack of gum out of her purse, unwrapping two and stuffing them into her mouth. She crumbled the little foil wrappers and dropped them onto the floor, much to his chagrin. "Thanks. You could have let me know you were here. I would have invited you backstage."

"Nah." Christa blew a quick bubble and snapped her gum, flipping on the radio. "Ashley wanted to go to the new teen nightclub in Houston, but I told her I was meeting someone, so I made her go without me." She blew another bubble, bigger, held it longer this time, her pink tongue searching, stabbing through the sticky mass and popping it as she turned the radio dial. "Besides, I wanted to surprise you."

"Well, you sure did." His knack for understatement had never been so pronounced.

She grinned, settling on some pop station he didn't recognize, her sideways look both knowing and a little shy. "The good kind?"

"Yes, sweetheart." He reached over to pat her hand, which was resting on the rise of her pale knee, hoping it came across as a fatherly sort of thing, rather than the lecherous creeper he was feeling like. The argument going on in his head was one any psychiatrist worth their degree would love to be privy to. He was thinking thoughts he knew he shouldn't let himself ponder. He was too drunk, too high on the night's performance, and still too dejected by his wife's rejection, to keep his thoughts at bay tonight. "It's probably not the sort of play your mother would want you watching, but I appreciate the support. I truly do."

"Meh." His stepdaughter rolled her eyes, tapping her feet in time to the song's beat on the dash. "We both know she's a prude."

"Christa..." He admonished her, but he felt her words more than heard them, a stab in his gut. Rachel hadn't always been like that, he reasoned. When they'd met, she'd been a little reserved, yes, had liked to make love (and called it making love, not having sex, never "fucking") in the dark. So she always liked him on top, so what? It felt just as good that way, didn't it?

When had they stopped having sex? He couldn't remember. Three months ago? Four? *Just before I'd sold my play,* he thought. Just before he'd begun to really take notice of his stepdaughter prancing around the house in sheer baby doll nighties, undressing with her door open, teasing him about not shaving by rubbing her cheek against his in the morning like a cat looking for attention.

"Not like Ashley's mom." Christa glanced over at him, smirking, and then repeated her earlier performance, mimicking Ashley's lusty mother. *"Ohhhh yeah, baby, stick that big fucking dick in me! Pound my pussy! Do it hard, make me feel it! Make me come all over your—"*

"Christa!" His cock was throbbing. Thank god their street was a dead-end road with few streetlights. He turned down it, seeking an even deeper darkness.

"Oh come on, Dad." She laughed, a light, breathy sound. "Those two were practically fucking on stage. They talked dirtier than that. And *you wrote about it.*"

He couldn't deny it. "It was an adult play. You really shouldn't have come."

"I'm an adult."

"Barely." He pulled into their driveway and cut the engine, feeling both relieved and let down at the same time.

"Old enough," she countered, turning toward him in the dark. Rachel hadn't left any lights on, inside the house or out. "How old was Crystal? Twenty? And Ben—he was, what forty-something? They were both consenting adults. Right?"

"It's fiction, honey." He took a deep breath, running a trembling hand through his hair. The engine ticked as it cooled, and the air in the car was already warming. "It's a play. It wasn't real."

"But it could be." Christa's words surprised him, but what surprised him more was the way she crawled toward him, across the gearshift, practically straddling it so she could press her mouth to his ear and whisper, "What if I want it to be?"

"Uhh... no... honey..." His cock didn't agree with him, not in the least, but he wasn't going to have that argument, not here, not ever. Fiction was fiction. This was reality, and this was very, very wrong. Even drunk as he was, he knew that much.

He could smell her gum—juicy, fruity.

"I know you watch me." Her words jolted him, literally, his body like a livewire. But she didn't relent. His reaction seemed to feed her intent. "I know you have a pair of my panties in your desk."

He groaned, shaking his head, closing his eyes, trying to deny it—but it was true. They were pink, one of the few

colored panties she owned, and he'd masturbated with his face buried in the crotch more times than he could count.

"I know you think about me when you jerk off in the shower." His stepdaughter licked her lips. He heard it more than saw it, the gentle click of her tongue moving from the roof of her mouth to trace the plump path of her bottom lip. "Do you think I come in to pee by accident? Do you think I don't know you're looking?"

Oh he looked. The sound of her voiding was enough to make his cock stand at attention, but it wasn't enough. He had to peek around the curtain and watch her reach behind—a good girl, wiping front to back, just like her mother taught her—wiggling on the seat, lifting her bottom a little, her tiny breasts almost visible under her tank-tee as she bent forward like that. He had splashed the shower tiles with his cum, loads of it, imagining her bent over like that in front of him, her behind rising up like an offering.

"I know it was about me." Christa's lips, sticky from her gum, touched his earlobe, and he felt her palm pressed between his knees on the seat, balancing herself. "I knew it the minute she came out on stage, the things she said and did. Thank god my mother didn't see it. Do you think she wouldn't recognize me?"

Would Rachel have recognized her daughter, fictionalized up there on stage for the world to see, seducing an older man who just happened to be her stepfather? She might have, he realized, with dawning horror. And then what?

"No, Christa," he said, his voice unbearably hoarse. "You have the wrong idea…"

"Oh no, I don't." Her hand moved, oh god, it moved up between his thighs, and he shifted in the seat, trying to hide the proof of his arousal. "I have the very right idea. The *perfect* idea."

"No," he whispered, but he barely heard himself. Her hand cupped him, rubbing deliciously as her mouth sought his. He couldn't resist, he simply couldn't. The soft press of

- 115 -

head to look up at him. "I'm so fucking wet. I have to play with my pussy!"

He nodded—as if she needed his permission—her words forcing more pre-cum from the tip of his cock. He hadn't been this excited since he was a kid in high school. To be honest, he'd probably never been this excited. Christa leaned in across the console, balancing with only one hand now, the other one pulling up her dress. He saw the flash of her white panties, and then he heard the most arousing sound of his life—the wet squelch of her fingers as she fucked herself.

"Ohhh sweetheart," he moaned, his hand in her hair, her mouth so soft, so slickly silky and yielding, he could almost imagine it was the hot clutch of her little cunt. Imagining that was almost too much. His balls tightened to the point of near-pain and he twisted in his seat, trying to hold it back, oh god, not yet, not quite yet.

She worked him only with her mouth, swallowing his length with greedy fervor, and the noises she made, her movements, drove him wild—the puff of her breath through her nostrils against his pubic hair, the way her hand, the one between his legs, balancing her over the console, moved between his thighs as she rocked, the impossibly soft skin on the inside of her wrist rubbing against his balls.

"Christa!" He cried out, trying to warn her, but she seemed to want it, almost as much as he did. When she pulled her mouth off him, just briefly, the change in sensation nearly sent him over the edge. But it was her words, those naughty, naughty words, that finally did it.

"Mmmm Daddy, my pussy is so fucking hot! Ohhh! I'm gonna make myself come!"

"Yes!" He thrust up, unable to hold it back anymore. "Oh honey, yes, come for Daddy!"

"Mmm! Mmm!" Her mouth and throat worked him, deep and hard and hungry, mimicking the contractions of her spasming pussy.

"Ohhhh! Fuck! Now!" The first blast shot out of his balls with such force it shocked him, his cock erupting like a volcano, bathing his stepdaughter's throat with a white hot lava. "Swallow Daddy's cum, baby girl! Swallow it!"

She did, eagerly, sucking hard, insatiable, as if she could empty him completely. He felt her trembling, her whole body aquiver, and caught her instinctively as she collapsed over the console, panting and laughing, her cheek resting on his leg, her shoulder against the steering wheel, where he noted her gum, still fragrant, was stuck fast.

"Christa, I..." The shame of what he'd done overwhelmed him. He wanted to apologize, to take it back.

"Don't you dare apologize!" She anticipated him, sitting up fast, brushing her long, tousled hair out of her face and licking her lips. Oh god, *she was licking his cum off her lips.* "Don't you dare, Daddy!"

He didn't. Instead, he went about straightening, tucking and zipping. He turned to her in the dark, wanted to reach for her hand, wanted to hold her, but didn't know if he should. She giggled, so young and girlish, and it made him smile.

"Listen I—" He didn't know what he would have said, but he never got the chance to say it, because the passenger door opened, startling them both.

"What in the hell are you doing?" Rachel demanded, standing there in her robe.

That was a good question.

"I... we..." He seemed to be great at starting sentences tonight, not so great at finishing them.

"Ashley wasn't feeling well, so I called Dad to pick me up." Christa lied so smoothly that Jim gaped at her in awe. She was already slipping on her heels, getting out of the car. He followed his wife and stepdaughter, too dazed to do much else.

"What are you doing in that dress?" Rachel asked as they entered through the side door into the kitchen. It hadn't registered, in the darkness, that Christa was wearing the

dress he'd left for her mother, but he could clearly see it now. "I was going to return it!"

"Oh, I didn't know." She sailed past her mother, heading toward the stairs, calling over her shoulder. "Me and Ashley were playing dress-up."

Rachel scoffed, calling after her, "You're a little old for dress-up, Christa!"

Jim sat at the kitchen table, more to get off his unsteady feet than anything else. His wife turned her attention to him, arms still crossed over her chest, her white satin robe bright in the kitchen lights, and he wondered if she'd seen anything. She would say something, wouldn't she? Accuse, rail at him, something.

"How was your little play?"

He blinked at her, trying to remember. Oh yes, there had been a play. He had written a play.

"Fine."

"Jim..." His wife leaned back against the counter, tightening the sash on her robe. "I've been thinking."

That makes one of us, he thought. He hadn't been thinking. Not at all.

"Yes?" He prompted when she didn't continue, rubbing his eyes, seeing lightning bursts and fading spiderwebs. He was going to have a hell of a hangover tomorrow.

"I'm leaving."

His head shot up, his eyes widening. "You're... what?"

"I need a break. *We* need a break." Rachel sighed. "I talked to Kathy on the phone after you left, and she invited me to her place in Florida for spring break. I booked the flight. It leaves tomorrow. I'm already packed."

"Well." What could he say? "If that's what you want."

"Okay. Good." She nodded, like it was all decided. "I'm going to bed."

He watched as she turned, padding barefoot past him. "Rachel?"

"What?" She stopped at the door, looking back at him.

He had a million questions and couldn't think of one. Finally, he asked, "Why wouldn't you come to the play?"

She sighed and shook her head, answering him cryptically. "That question is the very problem. Do you not know me at all?"

He sat back in his chair, wondering the same thing as she started out of the kitchen.

"Oh, Jim, please don't forget to feed Taffy, okay?" She peered back around the doorway to remind him.

"Who?" He blinked at her, feeling as if he was in a dream. Maybe he was just still too drunk to process any of this.

"Taffy." She pointed to the kitchen counter where her class rodent was busily shredding Kleenex.

"Oh." He gave a brief nod. "Right. Sure. Not a problem."

He listened to her climb the stairs. The house was so quiet he heard the familiar creak of the fifth step, the snick of their door closing. He should be devastated. Horrified. Panicked. Something.

But for some reason, all he could think about was his stepdaughter. He thought about her, upstairs in her room, how coolly she had handled herself, how composed she'd been. He thought about her mouth, her hands, her eyes, although he knew he shouldn't. His marriage was crumbling and he couldn't think about anything but fucking his stepdaughter—and his wife... his wife was worried about the fucking hamster.

That told him a hell of a lot.

* * * *

His office overlooked the backyard, which was a small affair, crowded with a little pond—ridiculous in the middle of Texas, the water constantly evaporating in the heat—and a huge trampoline. Christa used it regularly for cheerleading practice, and because he worked from home, he had the perfect vantage point for her after school antics. Today, though, Christa didn't have school.

He knew that spring break week meant both his wife and stepdaughter would be home with him all day, although this morning his wife had left for Florida and his stepdaughter had taken off in her brand new 2011 red Mustang convertible to meet Ashley at the mall, leaving him alone, which was how he usually spent his days.

Work waited while he brewed coffee, searched the Internet, dabbled on World of Warcraft for a while and even played a few rounds of Solitaire. He couldn't concentrate. Rachel had been in a better mood before she left, even kissing him goodbye and saying she'd call him when her plane landed.

"We'll talk when I get home," she'd whispered, hugging him tightly before getting into her Intrepid and heading off to the airport. He'd offered to drive her, but she had refused. He stared after her, still unshaven, standing there in his bathrobe, more confused than ever.

Before he knew it, the afternoon had rolled in, and he still hadn't touched any of his editing, although he had managed to shave and shower. That had taken far too long, because his cock had insisted on remembering the feel of his stepdaughter's hand and mouth, her velvety tongue and achingly soft lips.

Fuck. He was a bastard. A deviant. *Rachel was right to leave me*, he decided, trying to decode words on the screen in front of him, but nothing made sense. The Internet's siren call lured him and he found himself surfing and, clear admitted deviant he was, somehow clicking on a porn site. His cock made it to half-mast almost immediately, but the more he clicked, the more dejected he became. None of them looked like Christa.

And Christa was all he could think about.

As if on cue, the top of her blonde head appeared above the window ledge. Jim blinked in amazement, and then realized—she was practicing her cheers on the trampoline. Christa was so small and light that they used her to form the top of all their pyramids. He'd seen the girls during practice

on the few occasions he'd picked her up from school, his stepdaughter balanced precariously on a pile of female bodies, like the fine top to a trophy, or the goddess Venus rising out of a surf of flesh.

He could see her clearly enough. He'd sat back and enjoyed this show on several occasions, had even once let himself masturbate to the spectacle from the bathroom window when Rachel wasn't home. Christa in her cheerleading outfit was a sight to behold, all slender curves and jutting hips, the black and gold skirt so short it flipped up every time she leaped, higher and higher on the trampoline. Today she had braided her hair into two long, blonde pigtails on either side of her head, the effect of which was mesmerizing.

His window was closed—the air conditioning was on, because it was at least ninety-five out there—but he could hear her through the glass. She was cheering loudly, giving it her all, her pom-poms shaking, her feet first kicking out into a split, spreading so wide it made him dizzy, then she tucked them off to the left, her heels so high they touched her ass, then off to the right, repeating the delectable process again and again.

"Let's get physical!
Get down, get hard, get mean!
Let's get physical!
And beat that other team!"

Jesus.

Had cheers had gotten naughtier since he was in school? His stepdaughter whooped and hollered, shaking her pom-poms with fresh enthusiasm, and he found his eyes drawn to the yellow V at the crotch of her uniform under the pleated black skirt. She was like a tiny bumble buzzing around the yard, distracting him.

"Stronger than steel!
Hotter than the sun!
Jim won't stop
'Til he gets the job done!"

He stared at her, his jaw dropped, as she jack-knifed down on the trampoline, letting herself collapse into a fit of laughter. He watched her roll on the surface, giggling, finally lying still, spread-eagle, her skirt flipped up, the distracting yellow V between her legs taunting him. Her legs were pale against the black surface, her thighs slightly splayed, her knees sweetly rounded knobs, her shins smooth and shiny with sweat under the hot Texas sun.

She wasn't talking about him, of course. That's what he told himself. Some guy on the football team was probably named Jim. *It was a pretty predictable name for a quarterback at a Texas school,* he reasoned. Still, the gentle tease of her cheer, the way she sat up and shaded her eyes against the sun, looking up at his office window, as if knowing he would be watching…

Jim stood, closing his laptop and pushing away from his desk. He needed a break. What he really needed was a long, freezing cold shower. His cock definitely felt stronger than steel and hotter than the sun, that was for sure, and he damned well wanted to do the job. And he most certainly wouldn't stop until he was done.

Get a hold of yourself.

His cock encouraged him to do just that and he groaned, closing his eyes and resting his forehead against his office door, his hand on the knob. Then he straightened up, took a deep breath, and headed downstairs in search of some sort of distraction, whether it was a sandwich, coffee, or a nice, stiff drink would be determined by his state of mind by the time he got to the kitchen.

He stood at the fridge for five minutes before deciding, but once decided, the familiar action took over. For Jim, cooking was like meditation, and when Christa banged through the side door, he was practically zen. She shook her pom-poms in his face, making him sneeze, which only made her laugh as she tossed them on the table and toed off her sneakers.

"I'm starving!" she declared, peering over his shoulder. "Is that bacon? Oh my god, that's bacon!"

He lifted the paper towel he'd used to cover it to soak up the grease. "Help yourself."

"I'm all sweaty." She picked up a piece of fatty meat and chewed happily as he started to make his sandwich. "I need a shower."

"Glad to be on spring break?" He spread mayonnaise on his toast, arranging tomato slices, just so, totally in the zone. Christa was once again just his stepdaughter, and he was making an ordinary lunch, paying no attention to the way she peeled off her socks and wiggled her pink toes, the way she grabbed a greasy handful of bacon and sat at the kitchen table, thighs parted, skirt forming a U between them. No, he wasn't noticing the way she licked the grease off her fingers, the hungry little monkey, rubbing her plump lips with the tips of her fingers.

"Are we making small talk?" she inquired, raising her eyebrows as she watched him stack bacon on his lettuce. Zen. Totally Zen.

"Still making all As?" More mayonnaise on the other slice of toast. There. The perfect BLT.

Christa sighed. "Well, I guess small talk it is. Yeah, Mom was bragging just this morning to my dad about it. As long as I manage to pass my advanced chem final, I'll graduate valedictorian."

Jim nodded, bringing his plate to the table. This was the dangerous part, sitting so close. Their knees were inches apart under the table. "Speaking of your dad, I think he left a message on the machine."

"Oh I know, I talked to him this morning too." She grabbed his full milk glass, taking a gulp, and he watched her pale, slender throat work as she swallowed, the sight almost painful to him. She glanced up, seeing the look on his face, and grinned, the milk mustache on her upper lip making the expression even more endearing. "He called me

on my cell. Guess what? He broke up with what's-her-name."

"The dancer?" Jim bit into his sandwich, chewing thoughtfully.

"Yeah." She snorted, wiping her mouth with the back of her hand. "He's such a dick. I swear, you've been a far better father to me than he ever was."

Her words jolted him, and he felt both proud and guilty at the same time.

She snuck a piece of bacon out his sandwich, smirking, daring him to stop her. "Anyway, he's drowning his sorrows in the Florida Keys."

Jim stopped chewing, blinking at her. "Really?"

"Are we going to pretend last night didn't happen?" she asked lightly, but he felt her toes beginning to walk up his shin.

He ignored both her foot and her question. "Did you talk to your mother before she left?"

"Yeah." Christa shrugged. "She came into my room early this morning. She said she was going to stay with Kathy for spring break in…"

Her voice trailed off and her eyes began to grow wide.

"Florida," he finished for her, watching the same realization that had occurred to him moments before finally cross her mind.

"That bitch." Her whispered words caught him off guard.

"Don't you want your parents get back together?"

"I don't care what they do." She shoved away from the table, her eyebrows knitted, her face a storm cloud. "I only care about you."

"Christa…" He barely had time to put down his sandwich before she was in his lap, straddling him, her arms around his neck

"Take me to bed," she whispered into his ear, and he felt the press of her crotch, covered only with her cheerleader boy-short panties, against his. "Please. Take me."

She kissed him, full on the mouth, her tongue searching, probing, plunging. She begged him with her body—*take me, take me, take me*. How could he say no? He knew he shouldn't do it, he knew it, but he didn't care anymore. Right or wrong, he didn't care. Grabbing her hips, he lifted her easily—she couldn't have weighed more than a-hundred-and-ten—and, still kissing her, started out of the kitchen.

"Yes!" she cried, triumphant, as he started up the stairs. Jesus, he needed to work out more. She was light, but he was panting by the time he got to the top, turning toward the bedroom he shared with her mother. "Oh god, I've wanted you for so long."

"Me too," he admitted shamefully as she rained kisses over his neck, working the buttons on his shirt. She had them undone to his waist by the time he reached the bed, her slender fingers trailing over his chest, teasing his nipples, making his cock jump in response. He kissed her deeply, feeling her slip out of his arms, her body sliding down, down, down so she was sitting on the bed and he had to bend to keep his mouth fastened to hers.

She fumbled with the button and zipper on his jeans, breaking their kiss so she could focus on her task, shoving his pants down to his knees. His cock sprung up, hitting her lightly just under the chin, and she giggled, a delightful sound, grabbing him in her fist. She rubbed him against her cheek, her lips, closing her eyes and smiling, as if she could bathe herself in his pre-cum. There was so much of it, he thought maybe she could.

"I want to see you." He stepped out of his jeans, peeling off his shirt, and pushed her back onto the bed. She was still wearing her cheerleading outfit, but she was barefoot now. She stretched out on the bed, hands over her head, letting her knees fall apart for him, a tease. He saw the flash of gold under her black skirt, but he didn't want to start there.

"Take off your top." He instructed. His hand found its way to his cock. It insisted.

Christa did as she was told, pulling her uniform top up over her head, confirming what he'd assessed—she was braless. On her back, the buds of her breasts literally disappeared, leaving just the puffy rise of her pink-hued nipples. He groaned at the sight of them, his cock lurching forward, knowing just what it liked.

"Now your bottoms." He let her do it, because he knew if he touched her now, he wouldn't be able to control himself. She lifted her hips, sliding her uniform skirt down, catching the elastic of her yellow boy-shorts with her thumbs at the same time. He watched, fascinated, as she revealed herself to him, bit by bit—the wink of her navel, the jutting wings of her hipbones, the line of downy blonde hair at the top of her triangle.

Then she was pulling her legs up, giving him a view of her ass and that tight, puckered hole as she slid her skirt and panties up to her knees, over her shins, tossing them onto the bed. She smiled, a little shyly, her knees still together, off to the side now, her little body twisted on the bed. He thought he'd never seen anything so sexy in his life. Until she brought her knees up and let them fall open in front of him.

"Oh god." His cock didn't just lurch forward, it vaulted through his fist, aiming for the promised land, and he only stopped it by sheer force of will, inches from her glistening pink opening. The hair at the top of her cleft was dense, growing less so on the delicate wings of her labia. Her inner lips were pink and convoluted, hiding the bud of her clit, and his mouth literally watered at the thought of traversing that labyrinth.

"Spread it open for me." He watched her slim fingers part those lips, giving him what he wanted, a long, lingering look at the pink entrance his cock was aching to penetrate. But first, his tongue. He had to taste her.

Christa gasped and then moaned softly when he knelt beside the bed and buried his face into her flesh, like her pussy was a juicy, ripe peach. He couldn't believe her

sweetness. Her pale thighs quivered, the muscles on the insides growing more taut as she spread for him, offering more and more of her delectable fruit. He drank her in with relish, wetting his face with her juices, his tongue tracing the soft pink folds of her flesh, an intrepid explorer.

"Oh Daddy!" she cried, her hand moving in his hair, and he groaned at the reminder. This was his sweet little stepdaughter's pussy under his tongue, her hips thrusting up to meet him, her orgasm quivering, just at the verge of overtaking her. It was probably wicked, practically criminal, but that fact excited him even more. "Oh fuck! Daddy! Daddy! Make me come all over your face! Ohhh fuck, like that! Lick it hard! Harder!"

He grunted and brought his mouth down on her fully, lips fastened and sucking at the button of her clit. Christa bucked and cried out again and again, words he'd never heard her mother utter in the entire time he'd known her, words that made his cock weep with lust and jerk in his hand against the collar of his fist. She came and came, all over his face, just as she had promised, and he could have died right there and his life would have been utterly complete.

"Fuck me!" She insisted, pulling him up on the bed, but he was still too dazed, slow and full of her sweetness, so she pushed him onto his back, straddling him. "I want that fucking cock. I want you inside of me."

He just nodded, letting her, but he watched, like a dream, as she took his cock in her fist—Jesus, her fingers barely met around his girth—and aimed him. How often had he thought of this, imagined just this very thing? Countless, endless fantasies. And here she was, one little thigh out to the side to keep her balance, the tips of her pigtails teasing those delicious puffy pink nipples as she wiggled down toward his cock.

"Slow," he advised, knowing all too well that he just might explode instantly if she started like a racehorse out of the gate. "Easy, baby girl. Easy."

his tongue finding the sensitive spot at the top of her cleft, licking there, just there, swallowing her pussy juices in huge, throat-aching gulps.

"Oh yeah, that's it!" she gasped, rocking her hips just like she had on his cock. "Oh fuck, Daddy! You do it so good! Lick that hot little cunt! Eat it! Oh fuck, eat it good!"

His ears and face burned with her words and his cock certainly would have erupted right then if it had been receiving any outside stimulation at all. He even kept his hips still, tightening all his muscles to keep from shooting his cum all over the goddamned ceiling as his stepdaughter ground her pussy against his face.

"Coming! Coming! Ohhh fuck I'm coming, Daddy, ahhhhh!" And she was, shaking with signs and tremors that could have been mistaken for a seizure under other circumstances, her eyes rolling back, her toes curling, her teeth sinking so deeply into her lower lip he thought she might draw blood. He held her as she came, her climax fading slowly, with jerks and twitches, her eyes finally fluttering open again, only-half open, heavy-lidded and dazed.

"I'm going to fuck you." He tossed her onto the bed and she grunted as he grabbed her by her pigtails, both of them, pulling her ass up into the air. Oh Jesus, what a sight. Her pussy glistened in the afternoon sunlight, the blond hair beaded with her juices, her lips swollen and her flesh reddened from all his attention.

"Do it!" She looked back at him, her pigtails still in his one hand, her ass waving back and forth, a moving target. "What are you waiting for? Put it in! Fuck me! Please! Fuck me!"

"Tell me you want it." He couldn't resist. "Tell me how much you want it."

"Fuck!" She gave a frustrated cry. "You know I want it! Look at my fucking pussy! See how wet I am? I have to have your dick in me. Please!"

The sound of her begging was intoxicating. "Say please again."

"Please! Please! Please! Please!" She punctuated each one with a backward thrust of her hips, making her asshole wink at him.

"You asked for it." He didn't even aim, he just thrust, his dick finding its way as if equipped with sonar, sliding deep into the snug passage of her pussy in one long stroke. They both cried out at the sensation, Jim's hand tightening involuntarily on her pigtails, forcing her head back.

"Yes!" Her voice was hoarse with lust. "Ride me, Daddy! Fuck me good and hard!"

He couldn't stop. His brain turned off at some point and he became an animal, thrusting and rutting into her tender flesh. Christa didn't protest. In fact, she encouraged him, with vocabulary that would have made the entire Navy population of a nuclear submarine on leave from a two-month tour blush like schoolgirls. His stepdaughter begged him to fuck her, to do her, to ram her hot little cunt, and he did everything she asked and more.

"Ahhhhh baby girl, I'm gonna come!" he cried, grabbing both pigtails, pulling her head back and kissing her, hard, on the mouth. "Can I come inside you?"

"You fucking better!" she panted, squeezing his dick with the slick walls of her pussy. "Do it! Oh god, fill me with that hot load!"

Jesus. Fucking. Christ.

His cock blasted off like a rocket. If he hadn't let go of her hair and grabbed onto her hips, he probably would have shot himself across the room with the force of it. Christa rubbed herself off beneath him, but he was too far gone to think about it, except every sweet pulse of her cunt forced another blaze of white hot cum out of his dick, milking him until he thought he might pass out from the pleasure.

He collapsed onto the bed with a grunt, utterly shattered, and his stepdaughter mewed and practically purred as she curled up on his chest, like a kitten, not an inch of her body

touching the bed. His thoughts, when they finally returned, wandered to his wife, somewhere in Florida, likely hooked up again with her ex, who might have a taste for other women, but at least he, apparently, wasn't a pervert about it.

Unlike me.

He thought about his marriage to Rachel, how it had cinched progressively tighter like a noose around his neck until he couldn't breathe. He'd tried—god knows he'd tried—but could never bring her around to a place where sex with the lights on was a good idea, let alone entertaining things like dirty talk or oral sex. It wasn't that he didn't care about her, he did. But things had drifted, in such a short time, and he had to admit, it wasn't long after their wedding the little sprite sighing happily on his chest had begun to catch his interest in a myriad of ways.

Maybe it was perverted, but Christa made him happy. Perverted but happy. He could live with that.

She lifted her head, smiling dreamily at him. "Ha, this is just like your play."

"Happy ever after."

And that, he thought, tightening his hold around the delightful girl in his arms, *was just how life imitated art.*

Clara (Daddy's Favorites)

Clara wasn't as naive as they thought she was, but she let them all believe what they wanted. What did it matter? All the boys were either dumb, redneck boys whose idea of a good time involved beer and shotguns, or they were the kind of boys who drove muscle cars and dated cheerleaders from the town side of Otterville. She wasn't interested in any of them, so what did she care if they made fun of her for wearing overalls and muck boots to school?

She didn't care.

Not until they taped a sign to her back that said "Cunning Linguist"—she'd had to look that up online in the urban dictionary—because it just wasn't true. She liked boys—she just didn't like any of *those* silly, little boys. Still, they persisted. She went to retrieve an assignment from her backpack for a teacher and pulled out panties someone had stuffed inside like scarves from a magician's canister.

Then just today they somehow got into her locker—she suspected her locker partner, a chubby, unpopular girl who just might go along with a popular kids' prank just to be liked—and filled it with what had to be at least fifty dildos of all shapes and sizes. They spilled out onto the floor when she opened it to get her trig book after lunch, a well-timed stunt, because the halls were filled with kids, sluggish and lingering after lunch.

They all laughed of course. Clara heard Casey Kotter, head cheerleader, screech, "What's she going to do with one of *those*?"

The sight of Mr. Rosen tossing all of those fake dicks into a trash bag while she got escorted to the principal's office was probably the most surreal moment of her life, aside from the day she watched her mother carry a suitcase down their gravel driveway while the chickens bickered and pecked around her feet and their goat, Harold, tugged at the hem of her sundress. Clara and her stepfather had stood on the porch watching the procession. That, of course, hadn't stopped her. Clara's mother had thrown her suitcase into the back of a BMW while her young boyfriend—even younger than Grover, her stepfather and her mother's second husband—held the door like a chauffeur.

They called her stepfather into school, interrupting his deliveries—she could tell he'd been out on the truck and not out in the field because he was wearing good jeans and a clean shirt—and the sight of him sitting there in the little chair outside the principal's office, hat in his hand, head down, hangdog, like he was the one in trouble, made her heart lurch in her chest.

"Hey Grove—er, Dad." She tried to call him Dad in school or whenever an adult was present, but Grover was only ten years older than she was, and since her mother had married him four years ago, adjusting to thinking about him as her "father" had been weird. Not that he had ever insisted.

He looked up at her, nonplussed. "What happened, Clara?"

They hadn't told him? She sighed, taking the chair beside him and glancing at the principal's red-headed secretary, fingers clacking away over her keyboard. Mrs. Martin was nice enough and seemed sympathetic every time Clara ended up in the principal's office, and she probably knew what had happened anyway—the whole school knew—but she still didn't want to broadcast the latest event.

"Someone put a bunch of... stuff... in my locker."

Grover frowned. "What kind of stuff?"

She felt her face getting hot as she leaned in toward him. He smelled like the farm—they both did, all the time—but he was nice and clean for a change, and there was something else, a more fragrant, masculine scent. She felt him holding his breath as she whispered the words into his ear, "Sex stuff."

Then he sighed, letting out his pent-up breath, but they didn't have time to talk about it before Principal Brody was opening his door and waving them into his office. He'd called in the big guns, getting Mrs. D'Angelo, the school counselor, involved, and Clara sat in the corner, red-faced, and listened while they talked about "normal sexual development" and "homosexual curiosity" and "school bullies" and "suicide contracts" and when she looked over at Grover, she didn't know which one of them was redder.

But when Mrs. D'Angelo started asking Grover questions about Clara's mother, he stood up, jaw set and mouth drawn tight, still holding his hat, and said, "I'm going to take my daughter home now."

No one objected.

The ride back to the farm was quiet, even with the windows of Grover's Ford F-150 rolled down, the spring-almost-summer air cooling Clara's flushed cheeks.

"Do you want me to help you finish?" Clara glanced back at the boxes full of fruits and vegetables still stacked in the back of the pickup.

"No." He shifted into a lower gear as he turned down their dirt road. It was their road completely—there were no other houses or farms for a mile in any direction. "But I've got a family from the CSA weeding out back. Would you mind checking on them?"

"Sure." Clara didn't mind helping him. In fact, she loved it. She'd been the one to develop the website for Grover's Farm. She'd even suggested the name. The CSA—community supported agriculture—had been booming ever

since, and Grover's delivery area just kept growing. "Listen, Grove, about the, uh… the…"

He pulled into their driveway and cut the engine, cutting her off too. "Are you planning on killing yourself?"

"No!" She looked at him, horrified.

"Clara, to me…" He put his hat on the seat beside him and ran a hand through his hair. "To me, you seem like a very well-adjusted girl. Maybe I'm blind?"

"No," she protested, struggling to explain. She wasn't depressed or gay or suicidal or anything the school counselors—or her peers for that matter—thought she was. Everyone made assumptions, but no one ever really asked her. "I mean, you're not blind. I am. Fine, I mean. I'm none of the things they said. *None* of them. I swear it."

He nodded. "You've only got a few more months until graduation."

Her stomach dropped at the thought, even though she knew he was trying to reassure her. They hadn't talked about what would happen after graduation. Her mother had abandoned them both, and Grover had kept Clara on, even though he didn't have to, not legally. He'd never officially adopted her, and technically, she was eighteen, and could be out on her own right now. She'd made herself as useful as she could, but what happened when she wasn't in school anymore?

He put his hat back on, starting the truck up. "There's fresh chicken for dinner."

She knew that meant he'd butchered one just that morning. Sometimes she hated that part, but he'd long ago promised her one animal to "keep" and she'd picked Harold the goat. Everything else was being raised for food, and some chickens were for eggs, and some for meat. She just tried hard not to get too attached to the ones they were raising for meat. Besides, her roast chicken was melt-in-your-mouth divinely delicious.

"I'll roast it." She opened the door, snagging her backpack and sliding down out of the truck.

"Good girl." He gave her that sweet, shy smile that seemed reserved only for her and she wondered, not for the first time, if he was even aware of it. "I'll be back in two hours."

She watched him back out, guiding the truck down the driveway with practiced ease. It was weird—she knew she was weird—but there was nothing sexier than a man in a cowboy hat behind the wheel of his truck, backing it out the driveway. And she knew very well she shouldn't be thinking about that, especially in relation to Grover, as the heat filling in her face proved.

She found the chicken on a plate in the fridge and set about preparing it. Grover had missed a few feathers on the wings and she plucked them out by hand, rubbing the skin all over with butter and cutting up some apples and onions to stuff inside before putting it into the oven.

Then she washed her hands and headed out to the fields, taking a moment on the front porch to pet one of the barn cats. They were flea-bitten and some of them were mean, but this black and white one liked to laze on the porch on warm days, lazy-lidded, tail twitching, waiting for the sun to go down so he could begin his hunt for mice.

Out back, the family was coming in, the guys carrying crates full of weeds out of the field, and Clara felt something tighten in her chest as she watched the mother and father and two kids—a girl a little younger than her, and a boy a few years younger than that—laughing and walking together. The mother reached out and took the girl's hand, swinging it as they walked, and that tender gesture made Clara's throat tighten without warning.

"We put in a good hour," the father told her as they drew closer. "Where do you want these?"

Clara just nodded and pointed to the stack of crates, finding herself unable to speak. The families that joined the CSA had the option of buying a yearly share of the vegetables and fruit they grew, but they could also reduce the fee by offering to work on the farm. It was called a

work-share. Some of their clients did a full work-share, helping Grover year-round, and some did a partial work-share, like this family.

A sound from the barn—the high-pitched squeal of a piglet in pain—rescued her from having to attempt a conversation. Clara headed for the barn at a jog, waving to the family. "Thanks," she managed to croak, turning before they could see the tears. She wiped at them angrily as she rounded the corner and the sound of the piglet grew louder. Now the lower, gruntier sound of a larger pig had been added to the mix.

"Soooo-weeee," Clara called, looking through the wooden slats for the injured piglet. There were five of them rooting around in the mud by their mother, whose teats were stretched and raw from her nurslings, and none of them were paying attention to their missing sibling. But mama-pig knew—her head lifted and she called to her charge.

"There you are." Clara spotted the piglet wedged under one of the wooden slats in the corner, its bottom stuck fast in the mud. "How did you manage that?"

It was wiggling and writhing, but couldn't manage to get itself free. Clara sighed, grateful she was wearing her muck boots, as she deftly climbed over the fence and dropped into the mud on the other side. The piglets surrounded her immediately, nosing her and grunting noisily—they weren't exclusively on mama's milk anymore and they knew their food handler when they smelled her—but Clara ignored them, giving Mama a wide berth as she headed for the stuck piglet. If Grover saw her, he'd have a fit. Stepping into a pigpen was highly dangerous at any time, let alone with a protective mama pig around.

"Okay, little one, I've got you." She grasped the pig under the front legs, right around the middle, and pulled, but it just squealed louder in pain, surprising both her and the mama pig. Clara heard Mama grunt loudly as she got to her feet and knew she had to hurry.

"What are you stuck on?" she whispered, talking aloud to herself as she rooted around in the mud behind the piglet with her hand, searching for his back legs. She found the problem immediately—his hoof was caught in a loop of twine buried in the mud. The piglet squealed and flopped when she let him go, using both hands to try to loosen the string. It wasn't easy, not being able to see what she was doing, and the piglet made it harder, pulling and tugging the twine tight.

That's when she felt the mama pig's breath on her neck. Clara stiffened, working faster, her heart beating hard in her chest. She knew what it looked like, with the piglet squalling in pain and her hands on him, and she didn't blame Mama for being concerned. Clara had to move faster. She managed to work her finger between the twine and the piglet's leg, sliding it downward, and he fell free with a grunt, scrambling to his feet and squealing, probably in relief.

"See, it's okay, Mama," Clara soothed as the piglet sought his mother for comfort, already suckling at one of her swinging teats as Clara rose to her feet. The sow grunted, nosing her roughly, and Clara realized with a sinking feeling in her stomach that Mama was between her and the fence.

She moved slowly, edging around the sow and her surrounding piglets, ignoring the way her heart hammered in her chest. She'd never heard a pig growl before, but that was the sound growing in the mama pig's throat, and she wished Grover was here. He would have been over the fence in an instant to save her, she was sure. How many times had he told her going into the pigpen was dangerous?

"Easy, Mama, easy," she murmured, edging slowly closer to the fence, glancing sideways and trying to judge how fast she could scramble over the top. If the sow charged—six hundred pounds of angry pig—she just might be dead. Literally.

Clara felt it before it happened, something like electricity in the air, when the sow made her decision to move. She moved too, sprinting for the fence, praying she made it in time, zigzagging at the last moment, hoping to get out of the angry mother's beeline of fury. If Clara hadn't fallen, she would have been dead. The sow charged past her, just inches away, hitting the fence so hard it felt like it shook the whole barn.

Clara grabbed the fence, splinters gouging into her hands, and pulled herself out of the mud, scrambling up and swinging a leg over the top, falling with a grunt to the dusty barn floor on the other side. The sow squealed in frustration, rooting in the mud, sticking her snout between the slats, but her piglets were gathering around, squealing and snorting too, some of them rooting for milk, and now that Clara was on the other side of the fence, Mama began to lose interest.

"Stupid." She chided herself as soon as she could breathe again, sitting and checking herself over. Nothing broken, not even a cut or a scrape, aside from the splinters in her hands. But she was absolutely full of filth from head to toe. She considered going into the house, but the walk from the back door to the shower upstairs was long and even though the floors were wood, it would be a lot of extra cleanup. There was always the hose, but she shivered at the thought. It was a warm day for May, somewhere in the mid-seventies, but not *that* warm.

Then she remembered Grover's shower.

He'd rigged it up when Clara's mother had begun harping about the dirt he dragged into the house every day, up the stairs, to the shower. Even when he took his boots off at the back door, and eventually, started stripping down to his boxers there too, she complained, so he'd run a hot water line out behind the barn and screwed together some wooden pallets to create a shower stall.

Clara found a towel hung on a nail outside the make-shift door and a bar of Ivory soap inside. She glanced around before she started to get undressed, but even as she

did, she knew there was no one around for miles and it would be hours before Grover got back. The water grew warm quickly and she stepped in, soaping off not only the filth from her foray into the pig stall, but the nastiness of the entire day, from the horrible, dirty prank to the lecture in the principal's office.

They'd asked her over and over who she thought was responsible, but she wasn't going to tell them anything. Giving up her tormentors would do nothing but give them more ammunition, and even more reason to tease her. Instead she'd clammed up completely, letting the counselor do all the talking, while Grover looked between her and the adults with a bewildered, puzzled look on his face. The girl they were describing wasn't the one he knew at all. Of course that was true. The girl she was with him was the real one. Home was the only place she could really be herself.

Clara used the soap to wash her hair first, leaving her long, blond tresses squeaky clean. She usually braided it or pulled it back, but she hadn't today. She'd been up very early, before dawn, helping Grover with a mother cow birthing her calf, and had neglected to do much but grab her backpack on the way out the door that morning. She smiled at the memory, the struggle and mess and miracle of birth culminating in one very wet, braying little black and white calf who wobbled to his legs just moments after he came backwards into the world.

Grover had slipped his hand into hers, she remembered fondly, both of them bloody and full of goo, but what did it matter? He'd kissed her forehead and thanked her, and her heart couldn't have swelled any bigger for him. Clara slipped the white bar of soap over her belly, the muck of the pig stall and the darkness of the day swirling down the drain at her feet. She felt cleansed, renewed, her skin tingling and alive.

The soap traveled further down, between her thighs, and she scrubbed gently there, shivering at the sensation. They were wrong about her, all of them, so very wrong. She

wasn't a lesbian, or asexual, or uninterested in the opposite gender. She wasn't depressed—not really—nor was she suicidal or withdrawn or even shy. She was just... preoccupied.

And she wasn't about to tell them with what.

But even as her mind tried to deny it—and not just to her herself or her peers and teachers and the school administrators—her body knew just what it wanted. Her fingers took root at the top of her cleft, moving back and forth in the soapy wetness, sending warm waves of pleasure through her body. She couldn't help remembering the time Grover had first built this shower, before he'd rigged up the wooden pallet stall, and she'd stumbled across him using it.

Her mother had still been here then, she remembered— her mother was the reason for the outdoor shower in the first place. No more dirt in her house, she insisted! Her mother had forced Grover to wash off outdoors, even in the winter, and it had been winter then, the steam rising up out of the snow at his bare feet, his body revealed in the half-light of a setting sun, the strong, broad muscles of his back, still brown with a tan even in the middle of February, the sharp, angled muscles of his belly, and the rising tower of his cock between his legs, clenched tightly in his fist.

She'd retreated quickly back behind the barn, heart beating fast, mouth so dry she could hardly swallow, but she hadn't been able to stop herself from peeking again. She'd watched him, feeling ashamed and dirty, but excited too, as he stroked his hard cock with abandon, thinking no one at all was watching him. His head was thrown back, eyes closed, mouth a gaping "O" of pleasure, and his cock... oh god, the sight of it made her knees feel weak, and she'd had to hold onto the side of the barn to keep from collapsing.

But it was when he came that she actually did fall to her knees, because just as he thrust forward and exploded like a geyser over the rapid pump of his fist, he called out, not "oh god," or "yes!" or even her mother's name, which she might expect. No. Grover threw his head back and cried out, "Ohh

fuck, Clara!" as he splashed the side of the barn with streaks of his cum.

Nothing had been the same since.

Of course, she'd tried to not think about it, to pretend she hadn't seen. She'd risen to her feet, still trembling, and had run back to the house, staying in her room until dinner. But she'd never looked at Grover the same way again. And it wasn't long, months really, before her mother had told her she was leaving him, forcing her to choose. Not that it was much of a choice. The moment Grover said she could stay, her heart had decided.

Clara's hand continued to work between her legs, the soap abandoned on the ground as she leaned her cheek against the makeshift door with its hook and eye lock. The splinters in her fingers were forgotten as she rubbed herself faster, faster, seeing her stepfather in her mind's eye, imagining his big, hard cock not just in his fist, but in her own hand, in her mouth, oh god yes, buried deep inside of her. She sought to mimic the sensation with her fingers, pumping them in and out, seeing herself bent over in this very shower, Grover's hands gripping her hips as he drove hard into her.

"Ohhh god," she whimpered, breath coming faster, eyes clenched tight. "Oh yes! I'm going to come for you!"

And she did, trembling all over with the force of her orgasm, her knees weakening, just as they had that day, and she gave in and sank to them under the hard, hot spray of the shower, whispering her stepfather's name over and over. She knew it was wrong. She knew very well she shouldn't be thinking about him, fantasizing about him. But she couldn't help herself.

With a sigh, she picked up the soap and slowly finished washing, finally turning off the shower and opening the pallet door to reach the towel. It was rough but it served the purpose, and it was a little exciting to think Grover had dried off out here with this very towel. The slivers in her

fingers ached now and she looked at them, frowning. They were already turning red.

She spread the towel out on a pile of hay Grover had shoveled out of the loft, sitting down to see if she could do something about the splinters. The air was cool, but the sun was warm against her skin, and it felt incredible to be naked outside in the fresh air. She smiled as she reclined in the hay, giving up on her splinters. She'd have to go inside to get the tweezers. But for now, this was divine, resting clean and drowsy in a pile of hay, more relaxed that she'd been in months.

Her mind drifted. She didn't understand her mother and her decision, but she never had. Clara didn't remember her own father—her mother had left him when she was still a newborn. And she couldn't count how many "Dads" she'd had, although most of them had been "Uncles," to be fair. Her mother had married only two. Grover had been the last—and the longest. But that had ended too. When she closed her eyes, she could almost imagine him beside her, holding her hand and whispering into her ear. Oh he was so sweet, so kind and gentle and perfect.

"Clara."

She could almost feel his heat against her ear, smell the sweet hayseed of his breath. She squirmed and smiled and ached for him, reaching out with a sigh, wishing he was really there, solid and warm, so she could wrap her arms around him.

"Clara!"

She opened her eyes when her hands found the buttons of his shirt and found him kneeling above her, bent down with his mouth near her ear, a hand on her arm to shake her awake.

"Grover?" she whispered, blinking at the sight of the sun beginning to set over the tall grass. "Am I dreaming?"

"You must have fallen asleep. What happened? Your clothes are a mess... and..." He blinked, glancing down, his cheeks pink, and she remembered then that she was

completely naked. The look on his face was unreadable, but his eyes were filled with a sort of heat she could almost feel. How long had he been there? What had he seen? She felt redness creeping up into her cheeks as she sat, reaching for the towel beneath her and trying, rather unsuccessfully, to cover herself.

"What time is it?" she muttered, fumbling with the towel as Grover stood, holding out a hand for her. "I had to rescue one of the baby pigs and I fell. There—"

He exploded. "You went into the pig pen? Alone?"

"I had to!" She stood, wrapping herself up. "There was no—"

"No what?"

Clara stopped, eyes wide, finally registering what it meant—the sun setting over the horizon. "My chicken! Oh my god, my chicken!"

She ran. The towel fell off halfway to the house, and she let it, leaping over the black and white cat and bursting through the door to find the kitchen hazy with smoke. She coughed and sputtered her way to the oven, opening it to find a very black chicken inside.

"Oh crap!" She grabbed the oven mitts and pulled the roaster out, but it was far too late to save dinner.

"What the hell?" Grover came in behind her, coughing and propping the door open to let the smoke out.

"The chicken." Clara dropped the roaster on the stovetop with a clatter and burst into tears. "I ruined it."

"Oh Clara…" He took a step toward her and she sniffled, waving him away and wiping at her eyes with the big red oven mitts. That's when she realized she was still completely naked, standing in the middle of the kitchen, wearing just oven mitts. She looked up at Grover and saw the corner of his mouth twitching. "Don't you dare! Don't you *dare* laugh!"

"I wasn't…" He cleared his throat, tossing his hat onto the table. "I'm not…"

But the other corner of his mouth twitched and he started to smile.

"Grover Lindsey! If you laugh at me, I'll... I'll..."

"You'll what?" He chuckled. And that did it. It was like a dam burst. His chuckle led to a snicker. He tried to cover it with his hand, but it didn't work. Neither did trying to hide it in his chest. His silent mirth grew and inevitably escaped in great, whooping, knee-slapping guffaws.

"You!" She flew at him, not thinking at all, beating at him with her fists. He caught her easily, although he was thrown slightly off balance because he was still laughing so hard, keeping her from really doing any damage. "Ooooo! I hate you!"

"Oh Clara, you are too precious." He kissed the tip of her nose, her wrists still caught in his grip. That just made her madder, and she tried in vain to wiggle free, struggling so much it took her a moment to realize Grover wasn't laughing anymore. He was staring at her hands, a frown creasing his features.

"What in the hell did you do to yourself?"

She surrendered to him as he turned her hands over, palms up, revealing the splinters there. Before she knew what was happening, he had her upstairs in the bathroom seated on the closed toilet lid while he sat beside her on the edge of the tub with a pair of tweezers, pulling little pieces of wood out of her skin. But he did take the time to give her a towel to wrap herself up in, and she couldn't help notice the way he looked at her before she covered herself up.

"I've told you a million times not to go into the pig pen by yourself!" he growled, releasing his grip a little guiltily when she yelped at how tightly he was holding her. "What's the number one killer on a farm?"

She sighed. "Pigs. I know."

He tweezed and squeezed and removed all of the splinters she'd acquired during her piglet rescue, and then he got the hydrogen peroxide and the cotton balls.

"Clara, if I ask you something, will you be honest with me?" he asked, dabbing at her tiny wounds.

"Sure." She said it, but she wasn't sure if she would or not, depending on what he asked.

Grover put the cap on the peroxide and set it on the sink, tossing the cotton ball into the trash. His jaw was tight, and she wondered if she was in real trouble.

"Grove?" she prompted, watching his jaw work, his eyes distant, seeing past her. "Am I in trouble?"

"No." He focused on her again, smiling a little. "I just want to know. I need to know. Are you really a lesbian?"

This time it was the corner of Clara's mouth that twitched in amusement. If he only knew! "No, Grover. I'm not a lesbian."

"You swear?"

She nodded. "I swear. I like boys. I just don't like... *those* boys."

"Well..." He smiled, plucking her hand out of her lap again, blowing on her still-wet fingers. "You're young yet. I'm sure you'll find a boy you like one day."

He bent to kiss her fingertips, pressing them to his mouth, and she marveled at their softness, rubbing them slowly against his lower lip. His gaze lifted and their eyes locked and Clara felt her heart thump in her chest, her stomach dropping to her knees. My god, when he looked at her...

"I already have." Her voice was barely above a whisper.

"Oh?" He swallowed, not moving her hand as she traced her fingertip over his lip, down his chin where stubble grew in that hypnotizing cleft.

She stood before him, not much room between them in the little bathroom, so she was directly between his knees. He looked up at her, his expression dazed, a little like he was drunk, although she knew Grover didn't drink. Clara slowly, deliberately, began to drop her towel. His gaze followed the path of the fabric, pausing as she did before

revealing her breasts. They were pretty, pink-tipped, generous but not overly so.

She heard him inhale sharply and the soft sigh of appreciation that escaped his lips encouraged her to drop the towel a little further, over the soft curve of her belly, below her belly button, pausing again at the top of her hips. His gaze was fully on her, right there, and he was so close she could feel his breath against the peach fuzz surrounding her navel.

"Clara..." His tone was a warning, but a weak one, and she knew it.

She dropped the towel entirely and stood nude before him. He'd seen her sleeping this way out in the haystack, had seen her running like a crazy person naked through the yard just twenty minutes ago, but this was different. Entirely different.

"What are you doing?" he breathed.

"Proving it to you."

He blinked. "Proving... what?"

"That I like boys." She smiled, running a hand through his sandy-colored hair, already bleached by the sun. "*Men.* More specifically... *you.*"

"Oh god, Clara." He shook his head, his look desperate, trapped. "No... no..."

"At school, they taped a sign to my back. It said Cunning Linguist." She laughed, flushing red. "I had to look it up."

"Oh Christ."

"They meant cunnilingus. It was a play on words," she explained, unnecessarily. He clearly knew just what she was talking about. She could tell by the look on his face. "Oral sex. For girls. The funny thing is, I've never done that."

"Never?" Grover's eyes widened and he licked his lower lip as she ran her fingers lightly over his shoulders.

"No." She shrugged. "I didn't want to be like my mother. I tried that once. Didn't like it."

Grover cocked his head. "What do you mean?"

"I lost my virginity two summers ago at camp," she explained, starting to work the buttons on his shirt. He didn't stop her. "He wanted to and I thought, what the hell? Why not? But I didn't care about him... not really."

She paused, remembering. She'd known about sex, of course. It was hard to live on a farm and not know how reproduction worked. They had done what came natural, but somehow, it hadn't quite turned out the way she expected.

"Afterward, I felt..." She sighed, reaching his bottom button and pushing his shirt open to reveal the glorious sight of his chest and belly. "I felt empty. Still alone. And that's when I understood how Mama could just leave, like she does. Like she did."

"I'm sorry, Clara." Grover grabbed her hands when she reached for his belt. "It shouldn't be like that. It should be special. Beautiful. It should be with someone you love, who loves you."

"I know." She smiled softly, meeting his eyes, trying to show him with her look alone just how she felt. "That's why I waited. For you."

"Oh god, sweetheart." He shook his head, clearing his throat, letting go of her hands and grabbing her hips, attempting, unsuccessfully, to push her away—there was no room. So instead he tried to change the subject. "Listen, are you hungry?"

"Not for dinner." Her hands were free now and she reached down, daring him to stop her, and spread her pussy open at the top of her cleft, revealing the soft, pink inside. "Are *you* hungry, Grover?"

He groaned softly, watching her circle her clit with a fingertip. The sensation made Clara's knees weak, and doing it here, right in front of Grover, made it feel even better.

"I rub it a lot," she confessed breathlessly. "It feels so good. I rub it and I think about you."

"Clara no," he croaked.

She ignored him, closing her eyes, rubbing faster, a little faster still. "But I wonder what a tongue would feel like. It must feel so good. Does it feel good, Grover?"

"Yes."

She opened her eyes to look at him, asking, "Have you done it before? Do you like it?"

"Yes." He gulped, not taking his eyes off her pussy. She spread it wider for him and he groaned. "God yes."

"You like the taste?" She lifted her fingers and brought them slowly to his lips. He moaned, shaking his head, but she insisted and he succumbed, letting her slip them into his mouth.

"Oh fuck." He sucked gently on her fingers. "Sweetheart, you taste so good."

"Do I?" She reached down, curious, rubbing herself again and then raising her fingers to her own lips this time. It was tangy and left a slightly metallic taste in her mouth. But she liked it. "Mmm. Do you want to taste me for real?"

"Yes," he whispered, voice hoarse, expression pained as he watched her start touching herself again.

"Show me." She guided his head toward her navel with her other hand, pressing it down, down. "Please. Oh please," she begged. "Show me how good it feels."

He groaned and—finally—finally gave in, grabbing her around the hips and lifting her so her bottom rested on the edge of the sink. He peeled his shirt off, sitting where she had been seconds before, perched on the toilet, and spread her slender thighs with his palms.

"You're so beautiful," he murmured, starting at her knee and kissing his way upward. "Seeing you sleeping there today, I wanted you so much."

She brightened. "You did?"

"I wanted to take you right then and there," he confessed, rubbing his stubbled cheeks against her thigh, making her shiver.

"Oh, Grover."

He groaned as he neared her pussy, inhaling her scent. "I have to taste you."

"Yes." She ran a hand through his hair, pulling him close, anticipating the sensation, thighs trembling. "Please."

He parted her already-swollen pussy lips with his tongue and she looked down, watching more and more pink appear between the soft, golden curls of her pubic hair as he worked his tongue up and down her slit. He explored her slowly, making her moan in frustration. It was nice—very nice—but her clit throbbed, aching to be stimulated.

"Oh god your pussy is so fucking sweet," he moaned, shifting his gaze upward, meeting her eyes as he fastened his lips over her, focusing just where she wanted him.

"Ooooooo my!" She squealed and giggled and then a heat began to spread through her pelvis as he licked, licked, licked, his tongue flat and soft and utterly delightful.

He paused to ask, "Do you like that?"

"Yes!" She urged, shifting her hips forward, wanting more of his mouth. "Oh yes, lick it, please! Do it like that!"

He groaned, parting her with his fingers and flicking at her clit lightly with his tongue. "You make me so fucking hard."

"Show me," she begged, reaching for him, but he was too far. He sat back, undoing his belt and unzipping his jeans, shoving the denim down far enough to release his cock from his boxers. It was just as gorgeous as she had remembered.

"Oh yes," she whispered eagerly, watching his fist move up and down the length. "Stroke it for me like you do outside in the shower."

"Clara!" His eyes widened in surprised.

"I saw you jerking it for me," she confessed, putting her feet up on the counter and touching herself, unable to take her gaze off his crotch. "I heard you call my name."

"Oh Jesus." Grover reddened, but he couldn't seem to take his gaze off her crotch either.

"I touched myself afterward, remembering," she confessed further, rubbing her clit in circles. Oh it felt so good, but it was nothing compared to the softness of his tongue! "It made me so hot."

"Fuck," he swore, his hand shuttling up and down the length of his cock faster now. "I want you."

Clara let her thighs fall fully open, spreading her pussy lips wide. "Then shut up and make me come."

He groaned and dove in, licking furiously at her little clit, and she thought she might die from pleasure. Her body reacted without any warning, shuddering and trembling, every muscle taut and growing tighter by the moment, with every pass of his glorious tongue.

"Oh! Oh!" she cried, lifting her hips off the sink edge to meet his mouth, far up into the air. Grover grabbed her, wrapping his arms around her hips and throwing her legs over his shoulders so he could bury his face against her flesh, and he stood with her like that, surprising her so much she squealed like a little piglet.

He didn't say a word—he couldn't—but he didn't stop, mouth fastened tight, airless, over her pussy, his tongue lightning fast, driving her toward climax. She glanced into the bathroom mirror and saw he was holding her up with one arm. His other hand moved between his legs, jerking his cock in the same rhythm. His jeans and boxers were in a ball on the floor.

"Yes!" Clara grabbed onto his head, rocking on his shoulders, feeling her orgasm hovering, and worked for it. "Now! Now!"

She came with a force that shook them both, and Grover had to grab her around her hips with both arms then, steadying her against the wall as he mashed his face against her pussy. Clara shuddered, throwing her head back, and gave him everything, everything she had, everything she was, her pussy clamping down so hard she imagined if his cock had been inside her at that moment, she just might have snapped it in half.

"Oh god," she whispered as he let her slide slowly down the wall into his arms. She wrapped her legs around his waist, feeling the hard steel of his erection trapped between them.

"I want to be inside you." That was all he needed to say. His mouth captured hers and they kissed for the first time. Clara moaned into his mouth, sucking the taste of her pussy off his tongue as he carried her across the hall, kicking open the door to his bedroom. He put her down on the bed, the same bed he'd shared with her mother, but neither of them remembered or cared.

"Wait," Clara murmured as Grover poised himself above her. "Let me taste you first."

He groaned. "Not for long. I can't stand it."

That just made her want him more. She rolled on top of him, sliding down the bed to kneel between his legs. His cock stood straight up, leaking pre-cum profusely, and she looked up at him as she touched her tongue to the tip, saw the darkening look of lust in his eyes. Slowly she curled her tongue around the head of his cock, savoring the slippery feel, the peppery taste of his pre-cum, before taking him fully into her mouth.

"Oh god, Clara." He slipped a hand through her hair, watching her suck him. She was so desperate for him, a greedy little thing, suckling like the hungry calf they'd watched nurse for the first time that morning. Grover groaned, biting his lip and closing his eyes as she gave him a very wet, sloppy, exquisite blowjob, her lust matched only by his.

"I want you," she paused to whisper, rubbing his cock against her lips, her tongue, her cheek. "I want you inside of me. Please. Fuck me, Grover."

"Come here." He reached for her and she went, melting into his arms, their kiss wet and heated, tongues and legs twining as they rolled together on the bed. He shifted her onto her back, parting her thighs with his, his cock pressed hard against her aching mound.

"Please," she whispered, reaching down for him, but he caught her hand.

"Are you sure this is what you want?"

"I've never wanted anything more in my life," she breathed. "Fuck me. Do it. Ohhh god yessss!"

He slid inside, her pussy already wet and ready for him, and she felt his whole body tighten, heard his sharp intake of breath.

"Okay?" she whispered, nuzzling his neck.

"Yeah." He nodded against her shoulder, taking a deep breath. "You're just... so... fucking tight... it feels... ahhhh... so good..."

He began to draw back slowly and he gasped again, propping himself up on his arms to look down at her, drinking in the sight with his eyes. She saw him drowning in it, felt the swell of his throbbing cock inside of her.

"It's okay," she murmured, touching his cheek. "This part doesn't feel good for me anyway. You can come inside of me any time you want. I just like feeling you."

He smiled, easing back in again, nice and slow. "That's not how it's supposed to be. It should feel good for both of us. Do you like that? Feeling filled?"

"Yes!" She gasped as he pressed in deeper, as deep as he could go.

"Touch yourself," he told her, staying just like that, propped above her, and she looked down to where they were joined, the sight of him inside of her making her dizzy. "Do it, Clara. Rub your little pussy for me."

She whimpered, but his urging was too much to resist. She slid her hand down and began to circle her clit with her fingers just like she'd done earlier in the shower, fantasizing about this very thing. Grover watched, his cock throbbing, swollen, moving just slightly inside of her, almost imperceptible.

"Good girl," he murmured and she moaned when he bent to capture her nipple between his lips, sending bright hot flashes of pleasure between her legs. He suckled gently,

first one, then the other, the feeling of being filled by him so incredible, she thought she might burst.

But she wanted more.

"Please," she begged, her hips moving up, pelvis meeting his. "Please fuck me. Please. I want you."

"Rub yourself faster," he whispered, rocking and rolling his hips, teasing her from the inside out. He began to really fuck her and Clara cried out happily at the sensation, thrusting back up to meet him. Her pussy felt hot and swollen, so very full, and her clit ached.

"It feels good," she gasped, feeling a familiar tightness growing in her lower belly, something coiled, waiting to be unsprung. "Oh yes, you feel so fucking good."

"That's it," he panted, fucking her harder, faster, giving her more and more of just what she wanted—what she *needed*. "Do it for me, sweetheart. Come all over my hard cock!"

That was all the prompting she needed. Clara let her orgasm take her as her stepfather pounded his cock deep into her pussy, driving her pelvis into the bed again and again. She wrapped her arms and legs around him, lost in her own pleasure, but not so far gone she couldn't register his climax.

Grover groaned and thrust deep, his belly slapping one final time against her own as he came, filling her with his cum. The moment was so overwhelmingly sweet, Clara felt like crying as he slid out of her and she cradled his head against her breasts. There were no words for a long time as, outside, the sun melted over the horizon in a fiery display of orange and red, fading into deep blues and pinks.

Then they both heard Harold bleating.

Clara frowned, looking at Grover. The sound was very close. "Is the window open?"

"No." Her stepfather looked up as the little goat head-butted and bleated his way into the room. "The front door is though."

"Harold! Bad, Harold!" The goat had her remains of her muddy shirt in its mouth. She looked at Grover and they both burst out laughing.

"I love you," Grover whispered into Clara's ear, still chuckling, ignoring Harold's head butts against the side of the bed.

She wrapped her arms around his neck, unable to stop the tears stinging her eyes. "I never did thank you."

He lifted his head, propped up on his elbow, looking down at her quizzically. "For what?"

"Letting me stay."

"Oh Clara." He lowered his forehead to hers, closing his eyes. "I wanted you to stay. I want you to stay forever."

She brightened. "You mean it?"

"I've never wanted anything more in my life."

Harold settled himself on the floor, chewing happily on the edge of the bedspread while his master and mistress continued to do what came natural and this time it turned out exactly as Clara had always hoped.

Becca (Daddy's Favorites)

She was dreaming about him.

She knew it was awful. Twisted. Perverted. Even sick. It was so very wrong, on so many levels. But she couldn't control her unconscious, could she? And maybe that was the scariest thing of all.

In her dream, he touched her. Her mother was there for once, sitting in the living room on her laptop, smoking Pall Malls and swearing under her breath. She and Duncan were at the kitchen table, in full view, sorting slate from quartz from limestone from slag.

"Look, a Petoskey stone!" In her dream, she held it up, amazed. They were a rare find—both a rock and a fossil, the result of millions of years of glacial grinding and found only in Northern Michigan—and Duncan was just as thrilled as she was.

"Wow!" He admired her find, his eyes behind his glasses bright with excitement. And that's when she felt his hand on her knee under the table. The sensation was unmistakable, his palm warm, rubbing gently.

She swallowed and her dream-eyes met his. He'd never looked at her that way. She'd seen him admire other women like that, including her mother, at least way back when they were first married. And the other day, he'd been shocked into commenting about the new girl, who liked to wear short-short skirts and shirts that didn't quite cover her navel.

But he'd never turned to Becca with that look of lust in his eyes before.

His hand moved ever so slowly up her thigh, massaging. In her dream, she was wearing jean cut-offs, like she always did as much of the year she could get away with, and by the time his hand reached the seam of her shorts, she was so wet she was almost ready to come. And all the while, they both pretended nothing was going on, nothing at all. But she was imagining how hard his cock must be, and her pussy ached for release.

In her sleep, she whimpered, and she heard him say her name, a whisper so her mother wouldn't hear, his mouth close to her ear, and then she was coming, her orgasm a shameful, shuddering relief.

"Becca..."

She awoke slowly, still trembling with her climax, her own hand scissored between her thighs under the covers, feeling Duncan's presence beside her, his weight settled on the edge of her bed. Twisting toward him, she whimpered, unsure if she was awake or still dreaming until he spoke again.

"Becca, it's time. Are you ready?"

"Mmm," was all the answer she could manage, still too breathless to speak. Waking to find her stepfather in her bed after that dream was too surreal for words.

"Come on, sleepyhead." He brushed the hair away from her face in the dim light, and she saw through her window, just over his shoulder, that it was still dark. "The catfish are jumpin'."

"Comin'," she mumbled, flushing at her choice of words, glad for the darkness. "I'll meet you in the truck."

She got dressed in the dark, being quiet out of habit, even though her mother wasn't home. She'd left on another business trip last week, after being back for just three days, this time to some place in Europe. She'd called last night for her weekly check-in, informing them both that she wouldn't be in the United States again for another month. The plant

she was setting up in Italy was going to take longer than they expected.

Of course, Becca was used to her being gone. Her mother hired nannies to stay with her when Becca was little, but now she had Duncan. And Becca and Duncan had fallen into their own routine over the past two years, one more the norm than the times when her mother was actually home. She wondered sometimes if Duncan knew what he'd been signing up for when he married one of the most successful businesswomen in the country, but he didn't seem to mind. He was busy enough with his own business, building websites and developing Apps.

Duncan had the truck running and the heater on—there was a little nip in the air—and their poles and tackle boxes were in the back. The drive to the lake was quiet and quick. Becca shivered and Duncan turned the heater up even more, but she wasn't cold. It was an involuntary response. Her body just did things around him, without consulting her.

He parked and they moved like synchronized dancers, they'd done this so often, putting their poles and tackle into the boat, pushing it away from the dock, and hopping in barefoot, their shoes already in the boat. He grabbed one oar, she grabbed the other, and they began to row. The water was still and calm, like dusky, smoked glass.

They maneuvered the boat together into the current and Duncan slowly let down the anchor before they began baiting their hooks and tossing their lines. They each had two poles—double the chance for a whitefish dinner that night. She glanced over at him, wondering just how to ask him what she'd been so preoccupied with for the past week.

"You're quiet this morning," he remarked, as if reading her mind. He was still piercing his hook with one the night crawlers they kept in a cooler at their feet.

She anchored her pole, snapping it in place. "Just thinking."

"About what?"

She sat back in the boat, cross-legged and put her chin in her hand. "You know the new girl I pointed out to you?"

Duncan snorted, tossing out his line. "You didn't have to point her out. I imagine she gets a lot of attention."

"You can say that again." Becca sighed. "All the boys are after her."

"I bet they are."

"Is that really all a girl has to do to get a boy's attention?" Becca asked. "Wear short skirts and tight shirts?"

Duncan sighed, snapping his own rod and reel into place. "I suppose most boys would notice a girl like that."

"You sure did," Becca snapped, realizing how that sounded the moment it came out of her mouth.

"Well... I'm only human." Her stepfather smiled, pushing his glasses up his nose. He was very handsome, even with the John-Lennon-like spectacles that made him look a little too studious, with wavy dark hair and the most interesting gray eyes. They reminded her of the lake—reflective, expansive, wide-open and deep. "But just because they notice her, doesn't mean they really like her or respect her."

Becca laughed. "I don't think girls like Jessica want respect."

"That's probably true," her stepfather agreed, reaching into his pocket and pulling out a pack of gum. It was always the same—Dentyne Cinnamon Ice—and sometimes she dreamed about the smell of it. He offered her a piece, just like always, and she took it, tucking the wrapper into her pocket and the gum in her mouth.

"I wish boys looked at me that way," she said, watching the line of orange growing along the horizon as the taste of cinnamon exploded in her mouth.

Duncan frowned and shook his head, snapping his gum. "No you don't."

"Yes I do," she insisted, remembering how Jessica had flounced through the halls, her long tanned legs looking

even longer in impossibly high heels, her skirt so short it barely covered the curve of her ass. Her t-shirt was white with some logo on the front, but she'd been braless underneath, her dark nipples clearly visible. Even the principal, who had given her a warning about her attire, but who hadn't sent her home, had stared unabashedly at the way her nipples poked against her shirt. "Just once I'd like to turn heads like that."

"You're a beautiful girl, Becca." Duncan reached over, putting a hand on her knee, and she immediately flashed back to her dream, feeling her body fill with heat. "You don't need any of that to get boys to notice you."

"If you say so." She bit her lip, feeling his hand moving, oh god, just like in her dream, kneading her flesh, ever so slowly. *Yes, yes, yes,* she thought, bowing her head and closing her eyes in anticipation, letting her dark hair cover her flushed cheeks. She couldn't believe this was really happening, finally, finally...

And then he withdrew his hand, clearing his throat and fiddling with his rod and reel. "Any guy who's attracted to the Becca I know—the girl who likes baiting hooks and stalking deer and sailing—is going to like you for who you are. And who you are is pretty amazing."

She sighed. "If you say so."

"Trust me." He patted her knee, but his hand didn't linger this time. "Besides, if you ever leave my house looking like that Jessica girl, I'll..."

"You'll what?"

He gave her a dark look. "I'll spank your ass until you can't sit down."

"You got a bite." She gulped, nodding toward his fishing pole—the line had gone taut.

Duncan reached for his rod and Becca watched, dejected. She really didn't care about all the silly boys in school. Most of them didn't interest her at all. The truth was, the one guy she really longed to have notice her that way

was reeling in their first catch of the morning, and she didn't know if he would ever look at her that way.

But she desperately wanted him to.

* * * *

She'd spent an entire afternoon at the mall trying on outfits. Her job at the bait and tackle shop gave her some extra spending money and she'd been saving up for a new Mossberg hunting rifle, but right now, this seemed far more important. Her best friend, Ashe, had given his two thumbs up in the end. She couldn't remember how she and Ashe had become friends, somewhere back in the third grade, but he'd been her true companion ever since, and the fact he was gay—he confessed at some point in middle school—had always made things even better between them somehow. There was no pressure and it was easy to be the best of friends.

"You are going to knock him flat on his ass."

She'd cocked her hip and pouted. "Who?"

"Whatever guy you're doing this for."

"I'm not doing it for a guy."

Ashe had laughed. "You're the world's worst liar."

Okay, so it was true. But she wouldn't tell him who, even when he begged and threw a temper tantrum in the middle of the mall like the drama queen he was, threatening to leave if she didn't tell. It was the first thing in a long time she couldn't tell Ashe.

But he'd gotten over it by the time he picked her up for school on Monday. Duncan had a rare day off and was still asleep when she slipped out of the house. She thought wearing the outfit to school would work on two levels—it would throw Ashe off the trail, confirming it must be some guy at school she was trying to impress, and it would serve as a test run. If the boys at school looked twice, she'd know she hit the mark.

Turned out, it was a perfect bulls eye. Turned out, all a girl needed was a short skirt, a tight shirt that showed off some cleavage, and a lot of make-up to attract a boy's

attention. *Every* boy's attention, it seemed. So much attention it began to be uncomfortable in class. The girls whispered and glared, but the boys—guys who hadn't noticed her in cut-offs and Polos in an entire four years of high school—were suddenly boys falling over themselves trying to talk to her before and after class. She even managed to usurp the attention that had been heaped on the new girl, whose black cat suit-type outfit seemed tame in comparison to Becca's skin-revealing bits of cloth.

Every time she moved, she was aware of her body. The slip of her tank-tee strap, revealing an expanse of brown shoulder, the crossing of her legs pulling her skirt far too up her thigh—but not crossing them revealed the black thong Ashe had insisted she wear underneath the incredibly short, hot-pink skirt they'd chosen. Then there was the hardening of her nipples under her white tank-tee when someone opened one of the classroom windows—she could have sworn it was on purpose—which made her braless state even more prominent.

So it turned out her theory was correct—dressing provocatively got a girl all sorts of attention, turned heads and made everyone talk. As it also turned out, it landed her in the principal's office with a call home to Duncan to either come pick her up or bring her a change of clothing. That was after one of her teachers had given up trying to keep the class's attention off Becca's long, tanned legs in four-inch spiked high heels.

Duncan chose the former, showing up at the school with a scowl, following the principal into his office with another backward glare at her. She waited, head down, for the door to open again, her heart leaping to her throat when it finally did.

"We're going home." Duncan strode past her on his way out, but she'd already gathered that much.

Becca followed, struggling to keep up, unsteady in her shoes, the heels clattering on the tiles. He'd brought the truck, and she had to practically jump up into the passenger

side, something she wasn't used to. When she finally managed to get into the seat, she saw Duncan was watching her, his face slightly red, and she wondered how much she had revealed in her gymnastics.

She'd barely shut the door before he pulled out of the parking lot. Expecting a lecture, Becca tugged at her skirt, trying to pull it down to cover herself, but it was no use. There just wasn't enough material. Duncan glanced over at her manipulations, his gaze moving from her very short hemline back up to where she was trying to make the tank-tee cover her breasts.

"What in the hell were you thinking?" he snapped, shifting the truck into a lower gear as they rounded the corner to their street. Becca bit her lip and tried again, a futile gesture, to get her skirt to cover more flesh.

"I just wanted to see what would happen," Becca mumbled, regretting her decision now. It had been Duncan's attention she wanted to capture, after all, and while her mission might have been successful, it wasn't the sort of attention she had been after.

"You're going to find out," he growled, pulling into the driveway and cutting the engine. "Get into the house."

She slid out of the truck and wobbled up the driveway to the side door. She was hopeless in heels. How did her mother do this every day? Duncan was already inside, sitting at the kitchen table. His face was unreadable.

"Am I grounded?" she asked in a small voice, dropping her backpack to the floor.

"I told you what would happen if I ever caught you going out wearing something like that."

Becca stared at him, uncomprehending, but a dawning realization came over her as Duncan stood and began unbuckling his belt.

I'll spank your ass until you can't sit down.

That's what he had said—his exact words. Becca watched him unthread his belt, staring in disbelief as he

folded the thick leather over carefully, keeping the buckle in his hand.

"Come here." He snapped the belt and the sound made her knees weak, but she did as she was told, wavering only slightly, catching herself on the kitchen table. "Bend over."

She blinked at him in disbelief, her face reddening, and she cooled her cheek on the surface of the table as she bent over, feeling more exposed than she ever had in her life. His presence filled the room, rising up behind her, although she couldn't feel him, not physically. He hadn't touched her.

Every muscle in her body was tense as she waited, still aghast at her position, ashamed it had come to this. Behind her, Duncan was so quiet, it was unnerving. She glanced back, seeing his gaze on her standing bent over the table, a look on his face she'd never seen before, at least not when he looked at her.

It was pure lust.

Becca met his eyes, her own widening in amazement and a little fear. Duncan scowled, snapping the belt again, and she cried out when the first blow landed on her behind, part of the strap hitting her skirt, the other slapping hard against the exposed skin of her thigh.

"Ow!" She yelped, involuntarily shying away from him, but the next blow came fast and just as hard, this time on her other ass cheek. "Ow! Okay! I get it!"

"No." Duncan grabbed the edge of her skirt and yanked it up hard. She gasped and the belt stung her bare ass this time. "You don't."

Becca buried her face in her arms as he smacked her bottom again and again, her skin completely exposed, her black thong no protection against the blows, trying not to cry. It hurt—a lot—and her thighs trembled as she sprawled across the table, trying to get away, but she was trapped. Duncan punished her silently, but she heard him breathing hard behind her after the last slap of his belt had fallen.

"I'm sorry." His words were soft, almost a caress. And then, oh then, he touched her. His hand moved lightly over

the surface of her red and stinging behind, the best salve in the world. Becca moaned softly and arched without thinking. She heard his sharp intake of breath when she did, and then he was pressed against her, pushing her hips into the table edge.

"Becca, you have to promise me you'll never go out of the house dressed like this again." His voice was low, strained.

She sniffed, nodding, wiping her face—she couldn't help her tears after all—willing to promise him anything. Anything. "Okay."

"You are..." He cleared his throat, his hand moving in her hair, across the bare skin of her neck, through the valley of her shoulder blades. "You're a beautiful girl. You don't need all this..."

Becca gasped as his hands, both of them, moved to her hips, not just caressing but gripping, pulling her close. His crotch was right up against her ass, and she felt him. He was hard. So very hard.

And then he let her go, stepping away, turning around as he began to thread his belt through the loops in his jeans again.

"Go wash that junk off your face."

Still shaking, she did just as she was told, stripping down in the bathroom, taking off everything, including the thong and the heels. She got into a hot shower and scrubbed herself as if she couldn't get clean enough. Her skin reddened under the treatment, growing almost as red as her still-stinging behind.

She looked in the mirror when she got out, inspecting the damage. No skin was broken, no bruises. Her bottom was just hot and pink. She ran a hand over it, caressing herself the way Duncan had, and shivered. She'd seen the look on his face, had felt the steel-hard press of his cock against her.

Leaving all her clothes in the bathroom on the floor, she wrapped herself in a towel and went to her room.

Downstairs, she heard the TV on and the sound of Duncan banging around the kitchen, cooking something for dinner. It was like nothing had happened—except that her ass burned, and so did her cheeks.

And her pussy.

Her pussy was on fire.

Becca crawled into her bed, the towel falling away, the air on her skin cooling her hot, burning flesh. She buried her face into the coolness of her pillow as she stretched out on her belly, unable to stop herself from sliding a hand between her still trembling thighs. Her pussy was soaking wet, her clit thrumming under her fingers as she started to rub it. Closing her eyes, she remembered everything—the way he looked at her, the feel of his cock, so fucking big and hard against her crotch, his hands gripping her hips like he wanted to fuck her right then and there. *Had he wanted to?* she wondered.

She wished he had.

"Oh Duncan," she whispered, rubbing her little clit as fast as she could. She was so ready to come. Even in spite of the pain of her spanking, the way the belt had caught her sometimes had nearly sent her over the edge toward orgasm. She imagined him behind her, his cock pounding her pussy, and that thought alone would have been enough, but then she remembered how he looked at her standing bent over the kitchen table in her tiny little pink skirt, her tits on the table, her legs spread, and that sent her flying.

"Fuck!" she moaned, her clit throbbing under her fingers as her climax overtook her. "Oh fuck! I'm gonna come all over your hard fucking cock! Yes! Yes!"

She shuddered and rocked on the bed, burying her face in the pillow to keep from screaming at the force of it. It wasn't like she hadn't masturbated imagining Duncan fucking her before, but he'd never looked at her like he had today. That look of lust in his eyes made it more intense somehow—knowing he wanted her.

Becca sighed softly, turning her cheek, looking for a cool spot on the pillow, and that's when she saw the look in his eyes again, and it wasn't just in her imagination—Duncan was standing in the doorway. She was too surprised to do anything. She didn't even move to cover herself.

He cleared his throat. "Dinner's ready."

Then he was gone, back downstairs, and Becca finally moved to get dressed, a little too late. She yanked on a pair of clean, white, chaste cotton panties and a plain bra, pulling on sweats and a t-shirt before going downstairs. He'd made spaghetti and garlic bread, and he greeted her brightly as she came cautiously into the kitchen.

The whole meal went like that, as if nothing had happened at all. They cleaned up together, and Becca thought something might happen then, but they washed and dried in perfect sync with no incident. Then Duncan said he had some work to do and went upstairs to his room, leaving her downstairs in front of the TV, idly flipping channels, unseeing.

She couldn't see anything excerpt the way her stepfather had looked at her. Oh god, that look. She knew he wanted her. And she wanted him too. More than she could ever say.

So she decided to show him.

Upstairs, it was quiet. She stopped in the bathroom to pee and noticed her clothes were all gone. *He'd probably taken them to burn them*, she thought with a little giggle. She left her sweats on the floor, walking barefoot in just her t-shirt and panties across the hall to her parents' room. The door was closed and she stood on the other side of it, considering knocking, for a long time. The light was on, a slit under the door. What was he doing?

"Ohhhh yeah." The faint sound of his voice. She pressed her ear to the door, holding her breath. "Oh, Becca, suck it! Suck that hard fucking dick!"

Her eyes widened and she bit her lip as she pressed closer, trying to hear him, wishing she could see. Did she dare? Becca's hand tightened on the doorknob and she

turned it carefully, quietly, pushing the door open and praying it didn't squeak. She left it that way, just open a crack, catching a glimpse of her stepfather on the bed.

"Mmm that's such a good girl," he murmured—she could hear him clearly now—gripping his hard cock in his fist. Becca was so excited she couldn't breathe. "Suck it nice and slow. Yeah. Deeper... ohhhh yeah."

Was he really imagining her? Becca's pussy clenched at the thought, taking in the sight of him, completely nude, masturbating on the bed. When her gaze moved up to his face, her jaw dropped and she nearly gasped aloud. He had her panties—the black thong she'd left in the bathroom—up to his face and nose. No wonder he hadn't seen her open the door!

"Show me your pussy," he whispered, breathing deep into her panties. He looked different with his glasses off, like her stepfather, but not like him too. "I want to taste you. Oh god, I want to fuck you."

Becca bit her lip to keep from crying out at his words. *I want you too.*

What would happen if she went in? What would happen if she climbed up onto the bed with him and took that gorgeous cock into her mouth? Would he recoil in shock and horror? Would he push her away?

Would he spank her again?

Would that be so bad?

Becca pushed the door open further, getting a clearer view of him, cock rising up toward the ceiling, his hand pumping up and down the length. The sight of it made her mouth water. She pulled her panties off and left them on the floor, following quickly with her t-shirt and bra, and then slipping as quietly into the room as she could. The floor had thick, dark shag carpet and she was in bare feet, so she made it to the bed almost silently.

"Ohhh fuck, sweetheart, yes, like that, rub that hot little pussy for me." He was lost in his fantasy, eyes closed, the head of his cock glistening with pre-cum. Becca did as he

asked, reaching down and parting her soft, dark, wet pubic hair, fingers searching for the aching nub of her clit and rubbing as she watched him.

"Yes! Suck it! Suck my fucking cock!" He moaned, hips thrusting up as he imagined her mouth and tongue, and Becca couldn't resist. She leaned down and took him between her lips, groaning at the taste of his pre-cum on her tongue as she followed his fist down to the base of his dick.

"Holy hell!" Duncan's eyes flew open as he looked down at his stepdaughter, completely nude, sucking deeply and happily at his cock. He threw her panties aside as if they were on fire. "Oh! Fuck! Becca!"

"Don't make me stop," she begged, pushing his hand away and replacing it with her own. He was thick and throbbing and sticky with pre-cum. "Please. Let me suck it like you want me to. I *know* you want me to."

She rolled her tongue around the velvety soft head of his cock before working her mouth up and down, supplementing the sensation with her hand. Duncan moaned and shook his head, moving a hand to her hair, gripping hard—but he didn't stop her. And she wasn't stopping. She sucked him hard and long, breathing in his scent—he smelled cinnamony, like Dentyne, even there—as she worked his cock in and out of her hungry little mouth.

"You're so fucking beautiful," he murmured, and Becca gasped when his hand found her breast, squeezing and kneading her flesh. "Oh honey, wait, wait, that's so fucking good…"

Duncan pulled his cock out of her mouth and she whimpered, trying to capture him again between her lips. He shook his head, grabbing onto her hips and pulling her toward him, onto the bed. Smiling, Becca accepted the unspoken invitation, straddling him, anticipating his cock inside of her, but her stepfather had other ideas.

"Ohhhh!" Becca moaned when Duncan settled her not over his cock, but over his face, fastening his mouth on her mound. Sliding his hands up around her hips, he rocked her

on his tongue, teasing the little head of her clit so delightfully she had to grab onto the headboard to keep from falling over.

Her stepfather made soft, low noises in his throat as he licked her, sounding almost like he was enjoying it more than she was—almost. Becca's fantasy about her stepfather was coming true and she couldn't quite believe it. Was she dreaming? Could this possibly be happening?

She found herself lost in some surreal place, half-fantasy, half-reality, until sensation finally took over and she gave into it. Her pussy responded to his attention, her juices flowing down his chin, his cheeks, her labia swelling, and her clit pulsed deliciously against his flickering tongue. He was taking her places she had only fantasized about.

"Oh I'm gonna come," she whispered, slipping a hand through his hair. "Make me come, Daddy. Make me come all over your face!"

Her words made him moan against her mound and the sensation brought her climax to the surface like sudden the swell of a geyser. She flooded his mouth with her juices, crying out as she rocked her hips so hard the headboard banged against the wall over and over. He grabbed onto her, trying to hold her still, but she was like a landed fish in his arms, finally flopping sideways with a little scream, collapsing beside him on the bed in a sweaty, quivering heap.

"Holy hell," Duncan whispered, kissing his way up her calf, her thigh, parting her legs with his palms. She tried to resist—her pussy was still spasming with her orgasm, so sensitive she could barely stand it—but she couldn't resist him. She just couldn't. He was on top of her, kissing her deeply, and she could taste her pussy in his mouth.

"Fuck me," she whispered into his neck as he nudged against her with his cock, seeking entry. "Do it. Put it in. I want you."

Duncan hesitated, seeming to understand this was the moment of no return. She knew it too. "Are you sure, sweetheart?"

"Please." Becca's hips shifted up for him, seeking the perfect angle. "I can't think about anything else. I did it all for you. I wanted you to see me, to look at me... like that. I only ever wanted you."

He groaned softly, raining kissed down on her cheeks, her chin, her jaw line, her lips. "Oh Becca, you have no idea..."

She gasped, feeling the shift of his weight, the slow slide of his cock, spreading her open. "Oh!"

"I couldn't let you see," he whispered, buried, finally, deep inside of her. "How much I wanted you. I fought it every day. Every minute."

She tilted her head at him, eyes wide. "You did?"

"I can't fight it anymore." He began to move, making her whimper and shiver beneath him. He was so very hard for her.

"You don't have to fight it." She wrapped her arms and legs around him as they rocked. "I'm all yours."

"I love you, Becca," he whispered into her ear as he filled her, again, again, the slick slide of his cock sending shockwaves through her, his words filling her heart to bursting. She let him take her, his thrusts growing deeper, harder, driving her across the bed, and she clung to him with sweet desperation.

"More," she begged, moaning as his tongue bathed her nipples, first one, then the other, her pussy clamping down around his cock in response. "Oh god! Suck them! Lick them!"

He buried his face in them, still fucking her deeply, his cock battering her pussy, such sweet torture, making her pelvis buzz with heat. Becca gave him everything with complete abandon. Her body had no reservations about it, had always known what it wanted, and she wanted it too.

"Make me come," she cried, heels digging into the small of his back as he pounded her into the mattress. "Oh yes, Daddy, make me come all over your hard cock!"

And he did, his final thrust into her slick velvet sending them both over the edge. Duncan cried out against her neck, hips rolling, his pelvis grinding against her throbbing clit, her pussy snapping like a velvet glove around his pulsing cock. He shuddered and exploded into her, both of them clinging together. Duncan gave her everything she had ever wanted and more in that moment.

"Oh I love you," she whispered, kissing his cheek, seeking his mouth, finding it, sealing her words with a soft, wet cinnamon tasting kiss.

"What are we doing?" he asked softly when their mouths parted, although they were still joined together, inseparable as they has always been, doing this dance all along. "This is so... wrong."

"It's not wrong." She pulled him close, remembering how ashamed she'd felt for wanting him, knowing he must have felt the same. It wasn't perverted, or sick, or twisted. It was... "It's right. It's perfect."

He sighed, but it wasn't a sad sigh. It was full of relief—of *rightness.* "I'm so yours."

She knew it, somehow had always known it, but hearing him say it, seeing him finally, finally looking at her with all the love and desire in his eyes, filled her completely. This wasn't a dream, or if it was, she never wanted to wake up.

It was a dream come true, and it was all she'd ever wanted.

ABOUT SELENA KITT

Selena Kitt is a bestselling and award-winning author of erotic fiction. She is one of the highest selling erotic writers in the business. With over a million books sold, she is the cream-at-the-top of erotica!

Her writing embodies everything from the spicy to the scandalous, but watch out-this kitty also has sharp claws and her stories often include intriguing edges and twists that take readers to new, thought-provoking depths.

When she's not pawing away at her keyboard, Selena runs an innovative publishing company (www. excessica.com) and in her spare time, she devotes herself to her family—a husband and four children—and her growing organic garden. She also loves bellydancing and photography.

Her books *EcoErotica* (2009), *The Real Mother Goose* (2010) and *Heidi and the Kaiser* (2011) were all Epic Award Finalists. Her only gay male romance, *Second Chance*, won the Epic Award in Erotica in 2011. Her story, *Connections*, was one of the runners-up for the 2006 Rauxa Prize, given annually to an erotic short story of "exceptional literary quality," out of over 1,000 nominees, where awards are judged by a select jury and all entries are read "blind" (without author's name available.)

She can be reached on her website at:

www.selenakitt.com

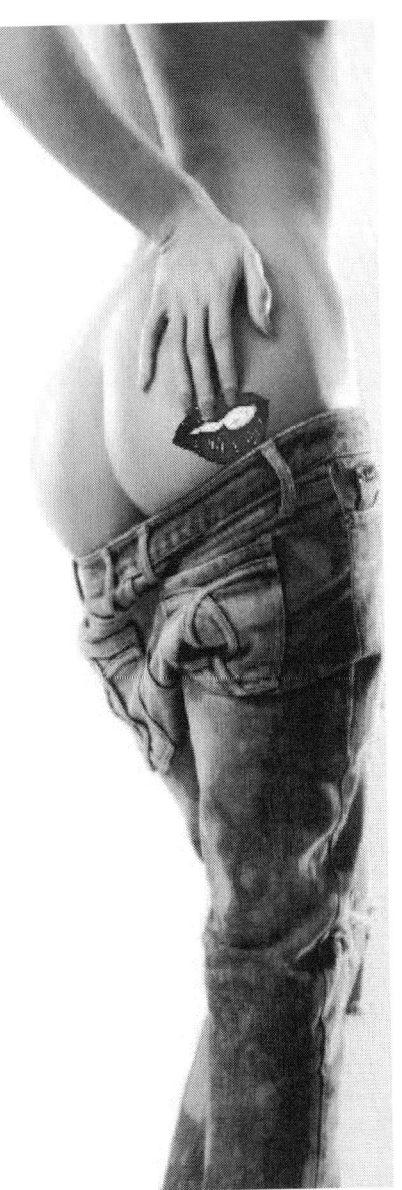

Made in the USA
Lexington, KY
23 November 2013